## SHOTGUN SHOWDOWN

There was a stirring of leaves and grass, faint as a lizard's rush, but Boot Lantry chilled, knowing instantly what it was, and instantly damning himself for being a fool. Mace Bracken was behind him, so close Lantry could now hear breathing.

"You turn and ride out, Lantry," Mace ordered, shoving his shotgun muzzle into Boot's back. "And if you reach for that six-shooter, I'll blow your backbone out through your front."

At these buckshot odds, Boot had no chance to fight back.

"That's right. Real good," cooed Mace. "You stand like a broke colt now and throw me your pistol."

"To hell with you, Mace. You want my gun? You take it!"

"Maybe I will. And maybe I'll take your life, too. . . ."

# THE BEST IN WESTERNS FROM ZEBRA

**THE SLANTED COLT**                                    (1413, $2.25)
by Dan Parkinson
A tall, mysterious stranger named Kichener gave young Benjamin
Franklin Black a gift—a Colt pistol that had belonged to Ben's
father. And when a cold-blooded killer vowed to put Ben six feet
under, it was a sure thing that Ben would have to learn to use that
gun—or die!

**GUNPOWDER GLORY**                                    (1448, $2.50)
by Dan Parkinson
After Jeremy Burke shot down the Sutton boy who killed his pa,
it was time to leave town. Not that Burke was afraid of the Sut-
tons—but he had promised his pa, right before the old man died,
that he'd never kill another Sutton. But when the bullets started
flying, he'd find there was more at stake than his own life. . . .

**BLOOD ARROW**                                        (1549, $2.50)
by Dan Parkinson
Randall Kerry was a member of the Mellette Expedition—until he
returned from a scouting trip to find the force of seventeen men
slaughtered and scalped. And before Kerry could ride a mile from
the massacre site, two Indians emerged from the trees and
charged!

**THE LAST MOUNTAIN MAN**                              (1480, $2.25)
by William W. Johnstone
Trouble and death followed Smoke all of his days—days spent
avenging the ones he loved. Seeking at first his father's killer, then
his wife's, Smoke rides the vengeance trail to find the vicious outlaws—and bring them to his own kind of justice!

**GUNSIGHT LODE**                                      (1497, $2.25)
by Virgil Hart
After twenty years Aaron Glass is back in Idaho, seeking vengeance on a member of his old gang who once double-crossed him.
The hardened trail-rider gets a little softhearted when he discovers how frail Doc Swann's grown—but when the medicine man
tries to backshoot him, Glass is tough as nails!

*Available wherever paperbacks are sold, or order direct from the
Publisher. Send cover price plus 50¢ per copy for mailing and
handling to Zebra Books, 475 Park Avenue South, New York,
N.Y. 10016. DO NOT SEND CASH.*

# BLACK POWDER POSSE

## BY ERIC ALLEN

Previously published in two volumes
as *HANGING AT WHISKEY SMITH*
and *MARSHALL AT WHISKEY SMITH*

**ZEBRA BOOKS**
**KENSINGTON PUBLISHING CORP.**

ZEBRA BOOKS

are published by

Kensington Publishing Corp.
475 Park Avenue South
New York, NY 10016

First printing: March 1985

Printed in the United States of America

# Chapter One

Five people were to tell for years how they saw him come a-riding, plunging his black horse down the south slope of Old Payne's Mountain, splashing across the brackish water of Garrison Creek and streaking out on the road toward Old Fort Smith.

Six persons actually saw him, but one of them was soon to die in gun smoke and a storm of scorching lead.

Only those close to the rider could have known he seldom ran a horse at that grueling pace, or that the big black had long since caught its second wind. The great horse was running with lowered tail, with a wild and flowing grace like a loping wolf that had already put miles of the Cherokee Nation behind him and was questing for plenty more.

The rider was giving the big horse every advantage possible, applying just the right amount of tension to the reins. His boots were thrust hard into the stirrups, and he was holding his wide, cream-colored Stetson, pushing his face and shoulders forward to streamline the southwest wind.

He was a big man, riding with a balanced ease, his high boots spurless. But the rush of the wind whipped back the tails of his long frock coat, showing his cartridge-studded gunbelt and holstered pistol. There was a deadly urgency upon him, plain for all to see.

Indian Joe, digging roots for winter medicine, saw him from where he crouched with his wife on the bank of the stream. Indian Joe dropped his digging fork and stared, open-mouthed.

"That dam' fine hoss!" the Indian said, squinting. Then he said, "Dam' big fine man, too, look like."

Indian Joe's fat wife had been so deaf for twenty years she couldn't detect a clap of thunder unless she saw the lightning flash. She sensed rather than heard Joe's talk. She paused in her digging, then shifted position and shook dirt from a sassafras root. Her black eyes measured Joe's eager face, his slack lip and shining glance, then cut around to fasten upon the rider in the distance.

"That fellar go down Fort Smith now, kill someone," she said. "That what I think." Suddenly her calloused hand snatched into a pocket of her checkered apron. A snuff box flashed in her palm. "Here, Joe. Shut your mouth and take good dip!"

"Old woman," Indian Joe said, reluctantly drawing his gaze away from the fast-moving rider and looking at his wife with fond amusement. "That thing you say would be hard for man, like divin' out creek to bluff!''

Indian Joe took the snuff box, then abruptly turned again to watch the rider and the running horse.


Wes Cutler saw the rider, too. Impatiently, Cutler hauled in his team of matched bays and sat tensely on the seat of the new Spaulding hack, lifting a gloved hand to shade his sharp eyes against the glare of the westering sun.

It was October. The wind already had a bite to it, but Cutler had been traveling fast since leaving Garrison Street in Fort Smith. With a savage and rankling fury against the lowness of the river, due to the prolonged dry weather, he had whipped the bays into a gallop immediately after driving off the ferry on the Cherokee side of the Arkansas.

Froth dripped from the bit rings that snugged close beside the bay team's flaring nostrils. In spite of the coolness, rivulets of sweat danced off their backs and withers and made round shot-droplets in the powder-dry earth of the road.

It had been a damnably dry year, Cutler thought for the thousandth time. The brittle, malignant shine in his eyes intensified. He was visualizing creeks turning as dry as old buffalo bones, the bones of starved cattle lining their twisting shores.

Only the spring-fed channel of Garrison Creek still had pockets of water large enough to quench the thirst of a good-sized herd.

Cutler pulled his breath in harshly, then expelled

it. He needed that Garrison Creek water. He needed it damned bad. And grass . . . up in the hills on Cutler's spread it was scorched gray as a wolf's hair. A man running beef needed much more grass, a hell of a lot more grass like that still growing on these bottom-lands, he thought. But how was a man to get it from the Lantrys, the family with one-eighth Cherokee blood who had ironclad rights to the land?

Above the hard breathing of the bays and the continued squeak and jangle of harness trappings, Cutler could hear the pounding of the hoofs of the oncoming black. Suddenly there sounded an ominous warning in Cutler's ears.

His oddly blue-tinged lips began to tighten. He pulled the team and hack off the road under the great arching branches of the sycamore trees and waited, hidden there while the rider on the black horse approached and passed.

There was fury in Cutler because he felt the need of pulling out of sight, but a man couldn't judge what might happen at any time or at any spot on this road to Old Fort Smith. Cutler's anger and impatience mounted for another reason, too. He could not see the rider plainly, could not recognize him through the foliage on the trees.

Sully Jansen saw the rider plainly, though, and he stiffened and sat a moment on his bareback pony on a trail that snaked off through the canebrakes from the winding river road.

Young Sully's thoughts were wrapped up more in stark reminders of recent weeks than of years gone by, but something about the rider on the black horse nudged memories alive in him. Sully watched the rider head into the curve just north of the old Sixkiller Graveyard, and fade out in a cloud of dust.

Moved by sudden impulse, Sully kicked heels into the ribs of his pony and galloped toward the cabin on the rise of land above Garrison Creek.

He had no intention of staying long at home. Hell with home, anyhow! But he could tell his sister Ina about that rider. Sully could also tell his sister some things he had on his mind.

He reined up near the stoop of the ramshackle cabin, turning to look again at the dust that was still rising on the road toward Fort Smith.


Ina Jansen had seen the rider through a window, a mere black dot-and-dash in the distance as he passed the trees that lined the road. The rider had drawn her attention like a magnet, and had worried her. It terrified her to see swift riders going past, ghostlike beyond the window pane. The hoofbeats of the black horse had made a disturbing racket, urgent as the tapping of a telegraph key.

It was a relief to her now when she noticed other movement near the creek and saw Sully riding up. Ina left some slabs of fatback sizzling on the cookstove and hurried out to meet her brother. She knew he was a renegade, but she loved him. She loved him as a sister should.

Sully leaped from his pony, his wide eyes gleaming, and climbed the stoop of the porch. His run-down boots skidded him to a stop, and he leaned close and whispered something in his sister's ear.

He heard her suck her breath in, and he moved back a step and watched her, his eyes ferreting like those of a wolf or weasel that was relishing the taste of blood.

"Oh, no!" Ina whispered. "Not him, Sully! It couldn't be. It just couldn't be!"

"I think it was," Sully said, and he kept watching his sister, because he was not the dumb kid folks had been taking him for.

Ina touched nervous fingers against the coil of blond hair at the nape of her neck. "Sully, do you think he knows we've moved from Fort Smith—or knows anything at all?"

"Maybe he don't now. But he will—and we didn't live in that damned Old Fort Smith. We lived on Cocaine Hill!"

Ina flinched as if her brother had twisted a knife in a raw wound. "Yes, on Coke Hill where you could run and hide every time you stole something from a store in town! Oh, that stealing you did was terrible, Sully!" She stopped and took a deep breath, and the light of dread showed in her mild eyes. "You know, Wes—Mr. Cutler—could have sent plans out over the telegraph. You know Wes is an important man."

Sully laughed derisively. "There ain't no telegraph across the Cookson Hills except what goes from mouth to mouth of outlaws. Lantry drove that herd up to the Verdigris country and he crossed the Cooksons to get there. No, I don't think he's heard about us moving from Cocaine Hill. I think Lantry is ridin' back fast because of something else."

"What is it, Sully? Do you know?"

Sully's eyes flickered again. "I know, all right. But

10

right now it's for you to find out!" He laughed and wheeled toward his horse.

"Sully!" Ina's voice was loud with urgency. "Sully, Mother has been wondering why you chased off to the woods to stay and won't live at home anymore. Why do you keep hiding out, like some animal in the woods? Why do you keep doing this way, Sully?"

"I don't like this damn country!" Sully said. "I don't like the work Pa tries to lay out for me. I'm gonna cross them Cooksons some day myself, and maybe join the Dakin boys!"

"Sully, you'll kill Mother if you do that! You know you will! Those Dakins—they're scum of the earth, just like Wes . . . Mr. Cutler said."

"Hell!" Sully blurted. "All I've been able to hear lately is what Mr. Cutler thinks! I'm sick of that. And as for Ma, she's already worried herself to the edge of the grave because Pa don't know how to take a-holt an' do things himself. He's always wantin' somebody else to do things for him. He's a snivelin' weaklin', Pa is, and allus was!"

"You shouldn't say things like that, Sully! Not about your father. And you ought to wait and see Mother. She's around somewhere, looking for late greens, I think. You ought to go look her up."

Sully spun about without answering, then paused an instant and looked at the dust where the black horse was still running. Then Sully grabbed the mane of his pony, swung astride, and soon disappeared in the woodlands along the creek.


Boot Lantry sensed signals of human attention,

knowing beyond the shadow of a doubt that people were watching him.

It had always been that way in these crime-infested hills and valleys of Indian Territory. A rider could not pass, day or night, unless people were aware of it.

Everybody watched everyone else. It had been even worse ever since the Civil War had brought divided loyalties, and all the murderers, rapists and robbers the other sections of the United States couldn't hold.

All along the Old Fort Smith—Tahlequah Road, women would rise suddenly from their pillows at night, listening breathlessly to the sound of hoof-beats. And men, white or Indian, would reach for rifles, pistols or shotguns, and wait, not breathing loudly, while the sound of the hoofs throbbed out of hearing either northwest or to the south.

If the caterwauling of a drunken Indian sounded, then the men with the guns relaxed. This was Indian country, a nation within a nation, but the Indians in it were the least dangerous of any who rode the trails or the wagon tracks.

That was the way it had been ever since all the riffraff, and the sharp connivers like Wes Cutler who hired them, had arrived in the hills west of the Arkansas River, Lantry thought.

But it was only a fleeting thought now, like the knowledge that people were watching him as he traveled. The rank, bitter currents of Lantry's thoughts kept swirling around something else.

A hanging. He had witnessed a hanging one time, right on the Federal courtgrounds in Fort Smith.

In his mind he could still see that bound and black-masked man, plunging through the gallows trap, just like old Jeb Fentress was doomed to do. . . .

Boots jiggling in a dance on thin air: imaginary freed arms fighting the rope—a man jelly-fleshed, goose-pimpled, death-sweating, snared by the gibbet loop.

Lantry slowed the grueling pace of the black horse as he neared the Sixkiller Graveyard. It wouldn't be right to pass the old family plot at such a rate of speed.

His mother, part Cherokee, a member of the Sixkiller clan, was buried there. So was Lantry's grandfather, the steely-eyed old Texan who had first married into Indian rights and started developing the land running cattle and fine horses in this region west of the Arkansas.

There were other Lantrys and Sixkillers there in the graveyard, too. Some had died in floods; others from fever; and still others from the bullets of bushwhackers during the Civil War.

It had been Lantry's part Cherokee mother who had given him the odd name of Boot. At the time of Lantry's birth, she had turned her eyes and seen an old cowboy boot standing in a corner of the ranchhouse. She had followed the ancient Cherokee custom, naming her second son for the first object she had seen while he was coming into this world.

Lantry's older brother had arrived in the dead of winter, on a cold night after the fire in the chimney had gone out. No Fire Lantry, this older brother was named. No Fire was married now, but living on the ranch with Pa, old Clint Lantry, holding things down along Garrison Creek and around the vast edge of Grassy Lake.

The force of the wind diminished as the black horse slowed. Lantry put on his wide-brimmed hat. The tails of his frock coat settled around his gunbelt and pistol. The sun, slanting down through the gum and sycamore trees, made alternating patterns of light and shadows against his face.

The trees in the cemetery appeared tall and stately, their leaves taking on a faint autumn tint against the cobalt blue of the sky. The branches of the gum trees threw large blankets of shade over the gray marble tombstones and the brown grass all around.

It was a focal point for tender memories, but there were other things nearby that flawed the picture it made. Lantry's gray eyes swiveled, fastening on the road forks, where the route split off through the bottomlands past a towering old tupelo gum.

On the tree he saw the yellow gash of the ax-blaze, with the pistol handle carved crudely beneath it, and the tattered reward posters hanging from rusty nails.

Lantry pulled the black to a standstill. He leaned sideward from his saddle, trying to read the reward posters, but their lettering was dim from weather and age.

A thought cut into Lantry's mind and he twisted around, looking for the road sign he had often read as a boy, while on his way to and from Fort Smith with No Fire or Ma and Pa.

The sign was still there like a garish challenge, the prong of an arrow pointing east toward the river and the border of Arkansas. The message on the old plank arrow was burned starkly deep and black:

FIVE MILES TO FORT SMITH. THE BLACK HOLE OF CALCUTTA. THE GATES OF HELL!

An impelling urge for action surged through Boot Lantry's veins. "Ho, Taw," he said tightly to the black, and ran a hand through the big horse's sweat-dampened mane. Lantry then swung a leg over the horn of his saddle and the next instant his boots made a plumping thud against the ground.

He felt the hurt from long riding shoot up through his feet and ankles, then slowly fade away. He walked close to the sign, holding the reins of the black horse, and stood there: a tight-lipped man, his aquiline features revealing the portion of Cherokee strain, his gray eyes narrowed reflectively, shadowed and deep with emotions stronger than he had known in years.

Then suddenly his right boot lashed out and the twin stakes that held up the wooden arrow broke at the surface of the earth. The sign hurtled end over end and finally came to rest in the dust.

# Chapter Two

Taw chuffed, his nostrils trembling, and suddenly side-stepped. A voice behind Lantry said, "Well, now you've come back on the prod, ain't you, Boot? Ain't it hell?"

Lantry wheeled, his right hand snapping back the tail of his coat and fastening on the butt of his pistol. His glance raked across the brush and saplings that lined the old cemetery fence. Just inside the fence he could see a straight-brimmed brown hat and the elusive face of a man.

Lantry's gun cleared leather instantly.

"Come out of there, Mace," he commanded. "What are you doing out here on our land?"

Mace Bracken laughed with a dribbled slowness, and it had the sound of pebbles dropping into a deep, dark pool. That laugh had always been a strange thing about Mace Bracken, like stones plopping into water, stirring ripples that spread and vanished, leaving the pool still and dark again. It was always softly reaching but ineffectual, and Boot Lantry thought now that no man or woman had ever been able to feel humor in it.

It was the laugh of an unfeeling killer. Mace Bracken would kill at the drop of a hat.

He stepped along the cemetery fence and reached the metal gate with its obelisk-topped sections, and came cat-footing into full view. In his right hand he was nonchalantly holding a shotgun. The sound of his progress was a bit puzzling until Lantry threw a quick glance at his feet.

It was a surprising thing, but Mace Bracken was not wearing the customary high-heeled boots. He was wearing shoes of a cheap cut and he was dressed in a cheap blue-serge suit.

Lantry had time for the fleeting conjecture that the change was purposeful, something to throw an opponent off balance and give Mace Bracken at least an infinitesimal edge. But that was an odd thought, too, because Mace could not have the edge. Boot Lantry already had his gun in his hand, leveled on Mace as the latter came through the gate.

Mace Bracken had aged some from hitting liquor, but he was still big and strong, and lithe as a catamount. His white buck teeth flashed in the afternoon sun.

"Yep, that was sure something to see," Mace said with galling derision. "A Lantry, losing his temper and venting his rage on a signboard. And wasteful doings, too. I never knew a Lantry to be so wasteful. Why, that there sign would have been good to use as a marker over Jeb Fentress' grave."

Boot Lantry watched him for several seconds without saying anything. Then he said, "Put down the shotgun, Mace. You tried to use one on me two years ago. I wouldn't want you to try that again."

Mace Bracken shrugged, then stooped and carefully laid the shotgun on the grass at the edge of the road.

"That don't rankle in me, Lantry," he said. "I wouldn't be about to shoot any man, no matter how much I hated him. Not here in these parts, where ol' Hanging Judge Parker stands so tall. You kill a man in Indian Territory now, you hang. That was what Jeb Fentress did. And he's going to hang."

"Jeb didn't do it, Mace."

"Hell he didn't. He killed Sue Bowman's daddy—left her a orphan child."

"Jeb Fentress wouldn't kill anyone," Lantry said flatly. "Old Jeb has been our foreman for at least fifteen or twenty years. I know his every quirk and fancy. Jeb wouldn't hurt a flea."

Mace shrugged again. "Well, any Lantry of the name would say that. It's because of Jeb's loyalty. I don't reckon your outfit ever had a man as loyal to your daddy's Hook Nine as old Jeb Fentress was."

Boot Lantry dipped his head. He holstered his pistol. "That's right, Mace. It's the reason we'll go to any measures to save his neck."

Mace Bracken had eyes with strange copper flecks in them; they could turn almost silvery and cold as chilled flint.

"There don't happen to be any measures, Lantry. Not in the jurisdiction of Judge Parker. No right of appeal, or anything. If you keep Jeb from hanging—

and it's just four days away—you'll have to tear down that dungeon jail and haul him away by force. And with a hundred or so deputy marshals now bunching in town, that ain't worth thinking about."

Lantry's voice had a whiplike quality. "I asked you a question, Mace. What are you doing, fooling around my parents' graves?"

"Why, I'm workin' for the Napier Funeral Parlor," Mace said. "I thought it my bounden duty to come out ahead of time and make arrangements about where we should bury Jeb."

Lantry's cold glance flicked again at Mace's town shoes. "So your Uncle Wes cut you off, did he? Took away your allowance and your whiskey supply, and you had to take the first kind of job at hand."

Mace Bracken's face began to blanch. Lantry could sense there was a curse on the verge of his lips, but it went unvoiced. Lantry's thrust had hit Mace—hard, hurting, raising the old hatred and fury that had been pitted against the Lantrys as long as Mace had been big enough to know what hatred was.

"I don't want to hear the name of Wes Cutler!" Mace growled. "I hate his guts worse than I hate yours!"

There was a faint reluctance in Lantry to push it, but he was remembering the gunfight that had left a saloon on Cocaine Hill a shambles two years ago. There had been a barkeep in it named Hemp Surate, but it had been Mace Bracken who had fired that shotgun from the doorway. Mace would have killed Boot Lantry, except that Mace had filled himself with too much raw-gut, and his aim had been so low most of the shot had ripped the floor.

Now Lantry said, "Well, Mace, your hating people isn't anything new. Fact is, I think you hate every living person on earth—except Mace Bracken, of course. Now move!"

"I told you, I rode out to—"

"I don't care what you rode out to do!" Lantry snapped. "If you step back into that graveyard, I'll stomp a mudhole in you and kick it dry. Start traveling! And don't ever let me catch you at this graveyard again."

A corner of Bracken's lips rose slightly. "This graveyard is not totally Lantry property now," he said. "There's the flesh and bones of the man Jeb Fentress killed right in there, buried not ten feet from your old grandpa! How you like that little deal?"

Lantry took an instinctive forward step. "Who authorized a thing like that? This is a family plot. Strictly that!"

Mace opened his lips and that laugh came through again. "Oh, there was some authorizing done. You bet there was! Because your pa figured Jeb Fentress was in a bind for sure, and that if he catered a bit to the family of Sue Bowman, maybe she wouldn't push the case too much. So your pa offered Miss Sue a good burial spot for old Tice Bowman. But a thing like that—or anything else—is useless when Parker says a man is going to swing!"

Deep in Boot Lantry's mind some questions were storming, but he wouldn't voice them. He wouldn't give that satisfaction to Mace Bracken, a man who had hated the Lantry family and had in return drawn Boot's contempt and hatred for years on end.

But what role had an old man named Tice

Bowman played here while Boot was gone? Where had the old man come from? Why had he been killed?

And Sue Bowman, this orphaned child Mace Bracken was talking about—where was she now? Was she a small child, with no one to adequately take care of her? Had her father been a wanderer in the Indian Nations, a traveling horse trader or drummer, crossing the Territory with his young daughter with him? Many a man, traveling across this land, had been killed from ambush, just as the message Boot had received had stated.

The message had been delivered to Boot by a stoical-faced Indian runner from Three Forks, where the Verdigris joined the Arkansas and the Grand.

"BOOT LANTRY, COME HOME. HELP SAVE JEB FENTRESS FROM HANGING. THE HANGING JUDGE HERE IN FORT SMITH HAS SENTENCED JEB TO DEATH FOR MURDER. FENTRESS SLIPPED UP ON A MAN AND SHOT HIM IN THE BACK."

The message had been unsigned, but Boot had hurriedly ridden off the isolated ranges to Fort Gibson, where a weekly newspaper editor had verified that Jeb Fentress at Fort Smith had been tried and sentenced for murder. So Boot had concluded the message had come from either No Fire or his pa, and that in their hurry, they had forgotten to sign it. Boot's fast ride on the big horse Taw had started then.

Mace Bracken had moved, and his move cut off Lantry's swift reflections.

"Don't do that, Mace! Don't touch that shotgun!"

Mace wiped a hand across his lips, then let his buck teeth show in a smile. "Why, I was just gonna take

22

my gun along, Lantry. You told me to go. I left my horse just 'round the bend. It's like I said: A man's a fool to think about killing someone, here in the Territory. You know something? Just last week the hangman, Maledon, dropped five men through that big gallows at one throw."

Lantry weighed it, watching Mace intently, gauging the light in his eyes, the expression on his face. Then Lantry placed his hand on the butt of his pistol and said very quietly, "All right, Mace, but you pick it up careful, and don't you face me. You just go on to your horse and ride out, because if you face me with that shotgun, I'm not going to be thinking about Judge Parker or the danger of hanging. I'm just going to shoot you down like the rotten cur you are!"

Mace Bracken's smile broadened slightly. He stooped and lifted his shotgun swiftly, not looking at Lantry. He spun about and went at a hurried walk around the bend beyond the weed-grown cemetery fence.


Lantry watched him go out of sight, then reached for the reins of his horse and walked slowly toward the gate of the cemetery. Always, after times away from home during his boyhood, his mother had rushed from the doorway of the ranchhouse to meet him with tears of joy and outstretched hands. Lantry wrapped Taw's reins lightly around a strand of the netwire near the gate, then took off his hat and entered the shady plot.

Lantry had ridden fast and hard and he was still in a hurry, but it would not be right to pass on by

23

without paying respects to Ma.

He heard the whistle of a quail somewhere close at hand as he stopped beside the tombstone, looking at the name: SARAH ELIZABETH LANTRY, 1832-1874. The quail whistled again, almost blithely, but then on the heels of it Lantry heard the distant and forlorn cooing of a mourning dove.

The October wind was cool against his face. He stood quietly, the knuckles of his hand showing tensely over the curled brim of the hat he held. Then he saw the freshly spaded earth and the new mound beyond Grandpa Lantry's grave, and he remembered what Mace Bracken had said. A faint resentment grew in Lantry because someone outside the family was buried here. That was a strange concession for Pa or No Fire to make, he thought. It was the kind of thing that would pleasure Mace Bracken and other enemies of the Lantry family and Boot Lantry was not inclined to give pleasure to Mace.

There was a stirring of leaves and grass, faint as a lizard's rush, but Lantry chilled, knowing instantly what it was, and instantly damning himself for being a fool. Mace Bracken was behind him, so close Lantry could now hear breathing.

"Your turn to ride out, Lantry," Mace's sibilant voice said. "You reach for that six-shooter and I'll blow your backbone out through your front. I don't like to be bested by you. Just turn around slow and walk away and mount up. I'm not finished with my business here. Haven't found the spot I want—a low and dirty and wet spot for old Jeb!"

A bluejay dipped from the branches of a red oak tree and swooped low above the tombstones, its beak emitting a raucous squawking that shrilled in Lantry's ears. The sound was like taunting laughter, daring Lantry to spin around, to draw and attempt to outshoot Mace, in spite of the buckshot odds.

Boot quelled the urge, knowing it would be futile. A man was a fool to allow either nerve or rashness to outweigh solid judgment. He stood still.

"That's right—real good!" Mace said. He stepped closer, his shoes cracking a mussel shell that hard rains, or perhaps the run of rodents, had rumbled from a grave. "You stand like a broke colt now and throw me your pistol"

"Hell with you, Mace. You want my gun. You take it."

Mace sucked in his breath and held it, then expelled it with a wheezing hiss. Boot had heard that sound from him before, back when they were boys in subscription school. Mace and his young thug associates had often ganged up on Boot and No Fire Lantry in slingshot brawls that had left the schoolgrounds a scuffed and bloody mess.

Always, just before the stones or rock-hard hickory nuts were whirled and hurled from the leather pouches to open the battles, Mace had held his breath until his face had become red and swollen, then had released it with that serpent's hiss.

Lantry felt the shotgun muzzle suddenly ramming into his back. A darting hand jerked back the tail of his coat and snatched his pistol from its scabbard.

"All right, now!" Mace said. Lantry heard the shuffle of his shoes going backward. "Get on that horse and light out!"

Lantry turned without even giving Mace the

benefit of an interested glance. He walked contemptuously past Mace and stepped out through the opening of the cemetery gate.

Taw was standing at the fence with his sleek head lifted, his big eyes as round and dark as obsidian pools, his ears flicking at Mace, then to Lantry. Boot unwrapped the reins deftly and tossed the right one under and over the horse's neck. His hand slid softly along the other until the reins met saddle. It wasn't until then that he gave Mace Bracken the full impact of his glance.

Mace had followed Boot from the cemetery. He stood at the edge of the road, his legs spread slightly, his town shoes planted in a blanket of dust that had been roiled up only minutes ago by the wheels of Wes Cutler's Spaulding hack.

The shotgun in Mace's hand was cocked, the muzzle pointing at Lantry. Mace had the stock of the weapon clamped between his hip and right elbow. Dangling nonchalantly in his left hand was Lantry's Colt.

# Chapter Three

Boot forced a smile and reined Taw around, bringing the big horse to a standstill, broadside in front of Mace.

"Well, Mace, it looks like it's your game."

Mace Bracken's buck teeth showed. "It sure does! It rightly does! And it sure does do me good."

"Yep. I figure it would." Boot tightened the reins of the black horse and settled in his saddle. There was resignation in the set of his head, the slant of his wide shoulders, as if there was nothing left to say and nothing to do except begin riding.

Taw lifted his right rear hoof out of a wagon rut and placed the shod hoof on firmer turf.

Lantry saw the grin broaden on Mace Bracken's face and noticed that Mace's thumb was easing back on the shotgun hammer, then gently letting it move forward until it struck the safety notch. Even the muzzle of the shotgun was lowered slightly. Mace's confidence was just that great.

The heels of Lantry's boots were squeezing in, and he knew that Taw was on the verge of rearing. Lantry could feel the muscles of the big horse bunching under the saddle, like hard-packed dynamite just waiting for the blast of the cap.

Boot's ripping command was the exploding cap that catapulted the black horse up and forward. With the first violent surge of motion, Lantry released the reins.

Lantry's hands smacked down at the same instant, jolting against the leather of the saddle swell on either side of the horn. He stiff-armed himself up in a gyrating twist as Taw bolted. Lantry came to earth with the litheness of a springing catamount, directly in front of Mace.

Mace Bracken's glance had involuntarily cut sideward, following the blurring streak of the horse. Mace was doing a frantic about-face when Boot's fist struck his mouth.

The sound of the blow smacked out above the noise of Taw's skidding hoofs as the big mount realized he was riderless. The horse wheeled around and stood snorting, his left fore foot mashing the tip of one of the trailing reins.

Blood stained Mace Bracken's lips and a snarl of pain and rage escaped him. He tried to right himself, dropping Boot's pistol and jerking the shotgun around into firing position with both hands.

Lantry's hat blew off as he feinted sideward, the taste of death already on his tongue. Mace was cocking the shotgun even as he swung it. Boot's sharp ears caught the sound of the deadly, warning snick.

To back up was to take the fanning impact of buckshot, possibly in the guts. Boot lunged in. He caught the muzzle of the shotgun and twisted it savagely downward between his widespread boots.

Lantry's bare head bored into Mace's chest as he ripped the weapon from Mace's hands, but not before it discharged. Lantry felt the muzzle bounce and flinched at the thunderous concussion.

Less than two feet behind him on the road the buckshot tore a chuckhole in a wagon rut and sent dust and gravel spurting into the elements. Lantry was straightening up, pitching the gun away, when Mace kicked him in the groin.

Pain screamed its way through Boot, running agonizing, fiery tentacles into every nerve and vein. The pain spilled from his eyes, from beneath his dark, slightly down-slanting lashes, but mingled with it was the slitted gleam of fury greater than he had ever known.

Mace was coming at him, jabbing with his balled fists and weaving from the waistline upward, and some of those blows were thudding against Boot's chest and shoulders as he stood his ground.

Then the first sickening run of pain was fading. Boot's left arm whipped upward, downward, blocking and covering. He set himself, then barely tiptoed and loosed a slashing right that tore flesh beside Mace's nose.

Mace backed up a step, his bloody lips spitting curses. He stepped on Lantry's gun. Mace's eyes cut down, and his body dropped as he squatted. His foot moved, and his right hand dug the dust in quest of the pistol butt.

Lantry stamped the hand and reached down to haul Mace upward. He felt Mace's fists sinking into his mid-section as they rose. Bracken had always been a hard man to beat, and time had not changed him. He was kill-crazy now, and if he couldn't kill Boot Lantry with bullets, Mace would try to do it with hands, feet, fists, or the iron-hard toughness of his skull.

Dimly, almost as if it was a dream sound, Boot heard Taw's muted, uneasy whinny. Then the sound rose shrill, trumpeting against his senses, and he knew another horse must be approaching along the Fort Smith–Tahlequah Road.

The sledging force of Mace's fist against his ear blotted out Lantry's concern for anything other than the urgency of the fight. This was one time, Boot knew, when he was going to have to bring into play all his strength, skill and strategy. Two years in the blind tiger saloons and Choc beer dives along the Arkansas-Indian Territory border had added considerably to Mace Bracken's stock of dirty fighting tactics. He knew all the brutal rough-and-tumble maneuvers that could easily maim or kill.

He was in close now, his left knee savagely thrusting at Lantry's stomach. The axlike edge of Mace's left hand was slashing toward Lantry's throat. Mace was trying at the same time to jab the stiffened thumb of his right hand into Lantry's eyeballs.

It was evident that Mace had come to the conclusion he didn't have enough wallop in fists alone to lay Boot Lantry low. Mace wanted to blind

Boot, then break his neck with that hacking hand against Boot's throat.

It was strange, but the knowledge of Mace's intentions honed Boot's thinking to a fine edge. Mace was coming against him in a straight-up position, and his face was clearly visible. Boot shot a left hook and felt the pain of the hammering impact streak through his knuckles as the blow thudded on Mace's head. The next instant Boot straightened, his right fist whipping in from just behind his thigh and crashing against Mace's chin.

Mace fell drunkenly, his head wobbling, and lay still in the road, sucking in globs of dust.

"You . . . you brute!" a choked voice said behind Lantry. "Did you intend to kill him? Is that what you want?"

Lantry turned, breathing fast, his face tight and his eyes still spilling out their harsh, fighting brilliance as he looked at the girl.

She was sitting on the seat of a halted buggy, less than ten paces away. The buggy looked new, its red spokes shining; hitched to it, rigged out in expensive harness, was a trim-built, little iron-gray horse with one albino eye.

The buggy and the horse were parts of the overall picture, but the girl herself dominated it.

She was fair of skin, and young, holding a wreath of flowers in one hand and the lines of the gray horse with the other. She was wearing a long black skirt and matching blouse and jacket; the jacket had white pearl buttons down its front. Her lips were full, her eyes as blue as the bluest pool on Garrison Creek, and rich whorls of black hair framed her features, spilling

31

from under the brim of a small straw hat with plumes.

For an instant she looked straight at Lantry, her glance stormy with anger, or scorn, or possibly both. Then she turned and looked down at Mace Bracken.

"Mr. Bracken!" she said. When he didn't answer or attempt to rise, she laid the wreath of flowers on the buggy seat, dropped the checklines, placed a high-button shoe on the step and came down. Again her scornful glance flicked at Boot. "Can't he get up?" she asked.

Boot rubbed his bruised knuckles. "No, ma'am. I don't think he can." Then he added, "If he gets up under his own power in less than two minutes, I'll have to take new stock of myself."

The girl said mockingly, "You're proud of your fighting ability, aren't you?"

"Yes, ma'am. I always was."

A tinge of heightened color rushed into the girl's cheeks. Her eyes lowered, then lifted swiftly, taking in Boot Lantry from the tips of his dusty boots to his full-cut, thick, black hair. Bare-headed, his face flushed with the pound of blood after exertion, he had more of an Indian look than usual.

"You're callous!" she said sharply, accusingly. She wheeled away and knelt beside Mace Bracken, lifting his head from the dirt and cradling it in her lap. She took a handkerchief from a pocket of her jacket and wiped the dust and blood off Mace's mouth.

Lantry watched her a moment, then turned and went to the roadside and picked up his hat. He looked at the hat intently, giving his whole attention to it, frowning at the smears of dust and grit on it,

32

affronted slightly as any pride-packing and discriminating man of the range would be. He slapped away as much dust as possible, then carefully creased the hat and put it on.

His long stride then took him to the spot where Mace had dropped his gun. Anger flared briefly in his eyes again as he stooped and got the big six-shooter. He stepped quickly to where Taw was waiting, and opened a saddlebag, pulling out a small roll of cotton cloth.

Lantry flipped out the cylinder of the gun, ejected the cartridges, and wiped both pistol and ammunition as clean as he could. He took his time at it, breaking off a section of a small wild cane stalk beside the road and twisting the cleanest portion of the rag around it to run through the cylinder chambers. Then he reloaded the gun and snugged it down into his holster.

"There'll be a next time, Lantry!" Mace Bracken's voice called out. "And next time you may not be so lucky, slippin' up behind me and tryin' to knock me cold with your gun!"

Lantry turned and saw that Mace had gained his feet, with the girl helping and bracing him. For a full half minute Lantry stared at Mace, his eyes narrowed, piercing, filled with contempt.

"Go ahead and get the lady's sympathy, Mace. Any way you can do it. But don't take too long. I've told you once to move away from here. If you let me close enough to touch you again, I may just break your neck!"

Mace swiped a hand across his lips, then opened them and started to take God's name in vain, which

33

was a definite habit with him, but he looked at the girl and apparently thought better of it. "You see how the Lantry clan works, Miss Bowman," he muttered. "It's plain to anyone."

The name Bowman got to Lantry, but he looked at the girl and didn't say anything. So this was the late Tice Bowman's daughter. Sue Bowman—the girl Mace Bracken had called "an orphaned child."

"You gonna let me take my shotgun?" Mace whined. He wiped more blood from his lips, making a show of pain and misery as he glanced at Sue Bowman. "You know a man ridin' in these parts has to have protection. That shotgun's all the protection I've got."

Lantry looked down at the weapon that was half buried in the dirt of the wagon ruts, and a trace of a smile lifted the corners of his lips.

"Yeah," he drawled. "Yeah, that's a fact, Mace. A man travels this road and a couple of bullies see there's no gun on him, and he's liable to just be hauled off his horse and maybe beat to death."

Mace started toward the shotgun, but Lantry raised a restraining hand. Slowly, deliberately, he ran the tip of a boot under Mace's shotgun and kicked it distastefully, just as he would have kicked a dead snake. The gun sailed all the way across the bar-ditch and landed out of sight in the rank weeds that lined the road.

Lantry heard Sue Bowman gasp. He looked at her and saw that her face was pale.

She said in a small voice, staring at Lantry, "I've never seen such a violent man in all my life!"

Lantry's face tightened. "Well, there might be

some question about that, ma'am. You've seen Mace, here, and there is not too much of a way to judge all the kinds of violence he packs." Lantry's glance lashed at Mace. "Leave the shotgun and get out of here. Move fast!"

Mace glared his hatred and passed Lantry, his face ridged and set straight ahead. He soft-footed through the weeds and tall cane and disappeared beyond a corner of the cemetery. Presently he reappeared, leading a bony roan. He mounted, turned once to look at Sue Bowman, then faced the direction of the river and rode away.

Sue Bowman abruptly went toward the buggy. Lantry took off his hat and followed her.

"Miss Bowman, I'm sorry about what happened. About your father, I mean."

She was taking the wreath of flowers from the buggy seat. She didn't look at Lantry or say anything. Her face was in profile, and there was a small girl look about it in the fading light that reminded him of the way Ina Jansen had looked once, when he had told Ina he would be going to the Verdigris country for a long while. A girl's face could wrench at a man, he thought, without her saying anything at all.

"If there's anything I can do, any way I can help you, I'll . . ." Lantry started to say, then his voice cut off. Sue Bowman was close, and he could hear the rapid sound of her breathing and could faintly see the quick pulsebeat in her throat.

Then suddenly she faced him. "Those are almost the same words your father said, when he offered to furnish the plot where Dad is buried," she said. "But after what you did to Mr. Bracken—a poor, defenseless man who directed my father's funeral . . ." She choked, then went on swiftly, "That was cruel, the way you did that. Cruel!"

Boot started to say: You don't handle a snake like Mace Bracken with cotton gloves. But he held it and watched silently as she turned and went through the gateway of the cemetery. She kept walking on the path through the grass between the graves.

Finally Boot caught up Taw's reins and mounted, but he didn't ride at once. He looked over the fence and saw the girl placing the flowers on the new grave of her father. She came out of the cemetery then, stepped up to the seat of the buggy, and began backing and turning the little iron-gray horse.

Suddenly it seemed intolerable to Boot Lantry that a person like her should be traveling alone on this route, with drunken passers-by almost constant, and outlaws hiding in the woods along the streams.

He reined Taw around, facing her. "Miss Bowman."

"Yes?" She checked the horse and buggy and looked at him. There were no tears streaming down her cheeks, but the sting of them was there, welling behind her eyes.

"Miss Bowman, would you mind if I . . . well, kind of side you, on your trip back home?" he asked.

"I don't need an escort—especially not from you! Is that fully clear?"

Lantry felt Taw shift restlessly beneath him. For an instant it was so quiet there was hardly a sound at all except for the faint squeak of Lantry's saddle.

Then he said, "You must be a total stranger to this country, Miss Bowman. Decent women don't ride the roads through here, alone."

Sue Bowman's firm chin lifted. "Oh, don't they, now?"

"No," Lantry said. "Some of the gun-toting hags like Belle Starr, now and then, but not girls like you."

The sun was behind her, dropping swiftly, and shadows were creeping across the valley, heralding night. He saw her shiver slightly as a gust of the October wind swept across the roadway. Overhead the crisp leaves of the trees made a racket like long-hoped-for rain on the distant hills.

"I could pick out a dozen men in this section," Lantry pressed, "and at least two-thirds of them would be renegades—men who rob and kill at will. That's the kind of country this is."

Sue Bowman's eyes were flashing at Lantry. "Almost everyone is a renegade and murderer, then? Like that killer, Jeb Fentress? The Hook Nine ranch foreman that killed poor Dad?"

She slapped the little horse with the checklines and drove on. The buggy wheels stirred thin sound from the dirt and gravel and the hoofs of the horse beat a steady tattoo around the turn and on toward Fort Smith.

Lantry watched her leave his sight, then followed, keeping a hundred yards behind. He knew he was going to keep riding behind her, at least until he saw her board the ferry. Once she crossed out of Indian Territory, Sue Bowman would be comparatively safe.

# Chapter Four

Indian Joe had lost interest in his root digging work and built himself a smoke out of the crumbly ground leaves of home-grown tobacco. He was conscious that his fat wife was giving him some impatient glances as she kept industriously digging, but to Joe those sharp reprimands from her black eyes were no never mind.

Indian Joe was going to take himself a rest.

He liked to sit cross-legged on the leaves of the woods and listen to sounds and watch things around him. He even liked to watch the knobby, calloused hands of his wife digging roots. It never troubled Indian Joe that his wife had to dig roots, or pick blackberries from the thorny vines, or pant and puff as she shinnied up a persimmon or paw-paw tree to get to the best fruit she could find. It was all right. She was Joe's old woman. She dug roots. She worked.

Indian Joe rested and smoked and watched things,

and when he saw human movement down the creek a short distance, he did not move or change expression.

It was that thin-shouldered, hungry-faced white woman that was always out questing for greens along the creek. She ought to know it was too late in the year to find much greens. But she looked, and her husband, head of the Jansen family that had moved near the creek recently, sometimes followed his wife and watched her as she searched for greens.

He was following her now, parting the branches of a thicket of alders. Indian Joe saw him, a squat-built man with a stubble of beard on his face, wearing patched shirt and trousers, scuffed shoes and a floppy-brimmed hat that was the color of dusty persimmon leaves.

The man was trying to overtake the woman this time, Indian Joe thought. He wasn't just following and watching her.

He was going to overtake her right down there at the creek edge, below Indian Joe and his wife.

Indian Joe scooted silently behind a clump of bushes and watched.

"Sara!" the man called. "Sara, you git back here and listen to me!"

The woman turned and looked back at her husband. Indian Joe's eyes sharpened a bit as Jansen approached her. It was plain that the white man was angry, very angry with his old woman, Indian Joe thought.

"Ina's gonna be gettin' herself in a bind!" Jansen said harshly as he came up to Ma. "I was watching th' road, and I saw Boot Lantry come back."

"Boot?" Ma said vaguely. Indian Joe, intently

watching, could tell even from that distance that her eyes didn't look right. They had a far away look in them, as if somewhere over the far hills, there was something holding her mind.

"Boot Lantry, dammit!" Pa Jansen snarled. "I just saw him go ridin' by like a bullet shot out of hell!"

"You oughtn't to curse that way, Tobe," Mrs. Jansen said.

"Curse?" His face looked furious. "Hell ain't a cuss word! Besides, I ain't no damn Holy Joe!"

Indian Joe's eyes narrowed, and he stayed very still. He could hear his fat, deaf wife, still digging away.

"I'd as soon Ina marries Boot Lantry as Wes Cutler," Jansen said. "Druther, in fact. I don't know why she ever taken up with Wes Cutler nohow. I don't think that man has got the money he claims to have. Why ain't he brung us some fat beef lately, or some good things to eat from town? When he moved us he said he'd take care of us. But he ain't done it. All he does is stop and sit on that hack of his and watch our daughter's pretty face. She is a pretty thing, that daughter of mine, I'll say that."

Mrs. Jansen looked at her husband without much interest, not half as much interest as she showed while she searched for greens, Indian Joe thought. Then suddenly she looked up the bank of the creek, and her thin hand lifted to point.

"Look, Tobe! There's a redbird. Look! They don't show as red as that very often, this late in the year, do they? Isn't it a pretty thing?"

Indian Joe grinned. A redbird was a redbird. A redbird was red just about all the time, unless it was part speckled, he thought. A bird was a bird. The

41

woods had lots of birds in them.

"I want you to listen to me, Sara!" Tobe Jansen almost yelled. "What I'm telling you is, there's likely to be some trouble, and it could happen in our front yard as easy as anywhere else. Nobody takes anything from them Lantrys! Not ever! A man steals a horse from them, or a calf or cow, and they'll hang him to the highest tree. By god, that ol' man Lantry, the old one that's dead and gone now, why, him and his boys hung killers and horse thieves a hell of a long time before Hangin' Judge Parker took the bench at Fort Smith!"

"I won't listen to your cursing, Tobe. I just won't do it," she said, pressing her hands over her ears.

Tobe Jansen leaped at her, snatching her hands down, shouting at her, spitting words into her face.

"If them Lantrys will hang a man for stealin' a horse, what you think's gonna happen when Boot Lantry finds out Wes Cutler is taking his girl? Our Ina, you hear? Why, Boot Lantry'll come and either kill Wes Cutler, or run Cutler out of the country. And then where will that leave us, I ask you? High an' dry an' starvin', that's where, and our Ina won't get herself a man that can maybe feed and clothe us. She's liable to miss the only chance she ever had of marrying a well-to-do man!"

Indian Joe was getting a bit puzzled, but he kept listening. You never could tell what a scroungy white man like Tobe Jansen might set himself to do.

"I don't care if Ina doesn't get married soon," she said. "I like to have her at home. She's a good girl, and pretty, too."

"That's what I'm sayin'!" Tobe Jansen raged.

"She's pretty enough she could get herself a man that was maybe rich enough to make life a little easier for us. But if she messes things up, we're ruined. I'll tell you, Sara, I don't believe Wes Cutler has got the money to keep payin' to graze his cattle on Indian land. Not for these dry hills that won't produce no grass. He's gonna run plumb out of water. And when he stops paying them crooked Indian agents, he's liable to get kicked out."

"You hush, now, Tobe. Go on wherever you were. I was looking for some greens for supper . . . maybe some sprigs of poke that I've kept cut back all summer long. Go on, now. Calm yourself."

Jansen stood doggedly staring at her. "Greens, greens, greens!" he fumed. "Woman, you ain't foolin' me! You ain't always traipsin' th' woods lookin' for poke greens. You're doin', all the time."

Behind the bush above the creek, Indian Joe sat a little straighter. He saw Mrs. Jansen turn and look at her fuming man, and there was something in her soft eyes that reminded Indian Joe of a hurt doe he had found in the woods one time.

"Yes," she said. "Yes, you're right, Tobe. I know there aren't any greens this time of the year. It's Sully I'm looking for."

"But he's a wild buck that'll never help us," Jansen declared. "Even if he married good, we'd never get any part of what he had!"

"I don't want anything except Sully," she said. "I want Sully to come back home and stay."

Tobe Jansen stamped a foot like an enraged stallion.

"That's because you've got your mind all warped

43

over that danged wild boy of yours!" he ranted. "Well, now, you'd better listen to me. Sully ain't ever goin' to be any good to us—not for anything. And we've got problems that lay any trouble about him in the ditch, I'll tell you that. It's like I said about Wes Cutler and them Lantrys. Them Lantrys have got just enough Indian blood in 'em to claim land rights, and they're smart enough to lease plenty more from the full-bloods that don't give a hang what happens from one sun to another, just as long as they can get their whiskey to drink. Them Lantrys are good managers, and they don't hit th' whiskey, an' I think it's high time you tell that girl of ours she better watch which side her bread is buttered on and begin butterin' up to Boot Lantry again, like she was two years ago. You hear?"

"You go on, Tobe. Go on, now," she said.

One of Jansen's hands darted up to scratch his beard. "You won't listen to nothing!" he flared. "Woman, let me tell you something. If you don't start listenin' to me, I may beat hell out of you! You hear that?"

Jansen wheeled and stamped away. She stood a moment, her fingers touching restlessly, then she slowly went on along the stream and vanished beyond a copse of trees.

Indian Joe took a long, deep drag on his cigarette, then ground it out in the dust. He never missed anything that was within range of his eyes, and he didn't miss the sight of the dust cloud that was rising again on the road that ran to Old Fort Smith.

This dust cloud was coming toward Garrison Creek. It was a team and a hack or wagon, looked like. Like the dust that had risen from the black horse that had been traveling in the other direction, this dust cloud now was moving pretty fast.

Indian Joe got up slowly, slapped the dirt from the seat of his pants, then stooped and raked the roots he had dug into the open mouth of a burlap sack. He took one squint at the lowering sun before turning and walking over to his woman. He reached down and slapped her on the back.

She jerked around and up, staring at him.

"We go home now," Joe said. He grinned, thinking of what Tobe Jansen had said, then added, "You don't listen to me, old woman, I maybe beat hell out of you!"

He had never before said that last part to his woman, and Indian Joe's wife could neither hear him nor read his lips. All she could see was the expansive grin on his face, slightly secretive.

"Joe," she said suspiciously, "you want get drink that Fort Town whis'!" She grabbed her sack of roots immediately. "You no do it. We go home."

They walked together, down the slope and across the creek.

They reached the road about the same time that Wes Cutler's bay team and hack came into view, close now, and still raising a lot of dust. Recognizing Cutler, a thought came to Indian Joe's mind.

"Wait, woman!" he said, and jerked her shoulder as he said it. When she saw the determination in his face, she stood holding her sack of roots, docile as a lamb.

45

Indian Joe dropped his sack and stepped out into the center of the road, both hands raised high, his long teeth flashing in a grin.

The bay team went sideward and the hack wheels skidded as Cutler slammed on the brakes. Dust rose in thick palls and settled all over Cutler. He stood up in the halted hack, a whip in his right hand, and glared at Indian Joe.

"Hi!" Indian Joe said, then in Cherokee, "*Cee-oo!*"

"What is it you want?" Cutler demanded.

"Want nothing," Joe said. "Just mak' stop, friendly talk. You want buy land?"

"Buy?" Cutler's brows drew down and his blue-tinged lips tightened after the word and flattened out. "Buy? How in the devil do you think I can buy land that's held in common? Buy the whole Territory? That it?"

Indian Joe jabbed a thumb against his chest. "Buy my land, water, grass for mak' cow fat! Hundred acre. Two. Woman here, she gots lotsa lan', too. We sell. You buy?"

"You're crazy!" Cutler snapped. He sat down and started to drive on by.

"My cousin, he chief—big chief," Indian Joe said. "Him like Lantrys—all chief! Him say, 'Cousin Joe, you want sell lan', buy woman fine dress, you good hoss, saddle, whis'?' You know, sell, mak' good time."

Very slowly, Wes Cutler lifted a neatly shined boot to the dash of the hack. The pupils of his eyes were like daggers, thrusting into Joe.

"Like the Lantrys, eh? And your cousin is chief?

He's competent? He doesn't have to ask an Indian agent what to do? That's crazy, fellow! You know damned well it is."

Indian Joe shrugged and turned and picked up his sack of roots.

"What do you have in that sack?" Cutler asked.

"I sell good grass, water, lan' to Lantry," Indian Joe said. Then he said, turning back to throw the weight of his sloe-black glance against Wes Cutler. "Them Lantry smart. They no say question 'bout lan'. They get chance buy, they buy. Mak' cow fat, put on steamboat, sell, get money. Agent not know when."

Cutler swallowed, and grimaced with the action, as if his throat were very dry. "Where is this land?"

Joe grinned and waved a hand expansively about him, "Creek here, big holes water, lotsa grass."

"I see plenty of grass, but I don't see much water here," Cutler said.

"Oh, that water, she up creek, beaver dam hole. 'bout mile. You want look? Come see."

Cutler swallowed again. "If I did look at this land and water, and it appears to be good, when could I drive a herd down and put them on it?"

Indian Joe set down his sack of roots and ran one hand up against his lower jaw. He turned then and said something rapidly in Cherokee to his wife. Her eyes looked blank, but when Indian Joe nodded his head, she nodded hers, then Indian Joe looked at Cutler.

"Sunup tomor'," Indian Joe said.

Wes Cutler's face showed amazement, then settled into a bleak calm. His eyes seemed to turn back into

47

themselves and become somber and inscrutable.

"How much money?" he asked.

"Oh, maybe hundred dolla, good hoss, saddle, graze four moons, then go 'way."

"Do you know how to sign your name to a legal lease form?" Cutler demanded.

"Oh, yeah, I learn write good," Joe said.

"All right," Cutler said. "I'll bring lease papers early tomorrow, along with the horse and saddle."

"And hundred dolla," Joe said. He grinned happily.

Cutler merely dipped his head in agreement, then rose and slashed the rumps of the bays with the whip and went splashing across the shoal of the creek and on up the swell of the mountain.

Indian Joe looked at his wife and grinned.

# Chapter Five

West from the river where Boot Lantry had watched Sue Bowman board the ferry, the road to the Hook Nine ranch headquarters edged the raw sunken wound of Grassy Lake.

Even in the twilight, Boot could see that the shallow water around the edge of the lake was scummy and stagnant. This was due to prolonged dry weather. Ordinarily there was a flow of water down from the highlands and the westward prairie, sending water through the lake fresh enough for cattle to drink.

A few bulls lumbered up out of the willows, their flanks caked with mud. Boot slowed the pace of his mount to gauge their weight. They did not look too good.

Then suddenly he became aware of a change in the land about him. There were cleared patches here and there, and a few scattered cabins that had not been in the region two years ago.

Always before, after short absences, when Boot had turned west on the road past the lake, he had been pleasantly conscious of how little the country ever changed. But this time it had been a long time. He knew some radical changes had taken place here west of the Arkansas during the past two years.

Boot frowned, aware of a growing annoyance. It was similar to the feeling he had experienced when he had seen the grave of a stranger in the old Sixkiller family plot.

Wherever he traveled, a man carried a picture in his mind of how he had left things in his homeland. He wanted to return and find that picture the same.

It was full dark by the time he had passed the lake and struck the uplands. Looking back, he could see the lights of the "Little Juarez" town of Moffett, and, eastward beyond the river, the stronger lights of Fort Smith.

He heard the forlorn whistle of a steamboat, too, and wondered if it was passing the mouth of the Poteau and the squalid little squatter's domain on the Choctaw Strip.

When he thought of the Strip and the huddle of shanties of Cocaine Hill, there was a tremor of excitement in him, and a vague, haunting sadness, too. It had bothered him for a long time that old Tobe Jansen didn't have enough getup in his nature to move the family to a better place.

Boot had met Ina Jansen in a summer twilight, sitting alone on the old Choctaw Wharf, her yellow hair in pigtails, dangling her bare feet in the water and looking with sad eyes down the long sweeping

Cherokee Bend.

The sight of her had tugged at Boot Lantry's heart and it had been the same with him ever since. He thought as he rode that after this business about Jeb Fentress was over, he would take Ina Jansen with him, as his bride, up to the Verdigris.

Boot rode into the ranch headquarters under the pale light of a crescent moon. Even before he reached the first corrals, a horde of barking dogs rushed at him, angry and clamorous. This was a puzzling thing. The Lantrys had never kept dogs that appeared to be savage animals, like these lunging shapes that were trying to nip Taw's heels.

The big horse wheeled and began to kick at them, nickering in protest. Then a man's voice commanded the dogs to silence and said, harshly, "Stay in that saddle, friend!"

It was the deep, threatening voice of No Fire Lantry. On the heels of it, Boot heard a pistol being cocked.

"No Fire," Lantry said. "It's Boot."

A sigh went out of No Fire like a great wind rushing.

"Damn, Boot, you shouldn't ride in here like that without warning!"

"Without warning? Shucks, brother, I've come home! Besides, weren't those dogs warning enough? What's going on here?"

"Nothing we can't handle . . . maybe," No Fire answered. He materialized from a nearby shed, and in the moonlight Boot could see he was offering his hand. Boot took it and felt the warmth surge through him, the old family closeness that noth-

51

ing could shake.

No Fire turned to the corral gate and there was a time of waiting. Boot wondered about it, then realized that No Fire was fumbling with a padlock and a chain. Then the gate swung open. Within a few minutes Taw's needs were taken care of and Boot and No Fire were walking toward the house.

It was comparatively early, but the ranchhouse was already darkened and quiet. Ordinarily the front door would have opened at first sound of their footsteps, and Pa's face with its gray burnsides and long white moustache would have peered out. But it wasn't that way on this night. The door wasn't opened until No Fire said, "It's all right, Pa. It's Boot."

Then Pa stood there; crowding close behind him was No Fire's comely part-Cherokee wife, Lawana. As he shook hands with them Boot looked around the room and realized that candles had been burning all the time. Heavy blinds at all the windows, drawn tightly, had sealed in the light.

"Good to see you, son," old Clint Lantry said. That was all he said at first. They had never been a demonstrative family. But Lawana's attitude of fear got to Boot. Her great dark eyes were luminous, very close to tears, he thought. That was strange, for a woman as much Indian as she.

"You eaten yet, son?" Clint asked.

"Not on your tintype!" Boot said. He walked to the fireplace where a small blaze was going and turned his back to it, then faced them with a smile. There ought to be more cheer in this house, he thought. "But my appetite went down a notch after those vicious dogs attacked. I was about to shoot them."

"We need dogs now," Clint said. "Some prowlers at night."

Boot turned to Lawana. "Stir up some chuck, sis-in-law, before I wham you good," he said, and watched a smile touch her lips briefly before she went through the kitchen door. The family talk would begin after he had eaten.

A half hour later Boot had eaten and the family was gathered in comfortable chairs in front of the fire. Things began to come out into the open with several jolting impacts, fact after fact.

"There's no way to defend old Jeb," Clint said. "He swears he did that killing. Even declares he shot Tice Bowman in the back."

Boot looked from Clint to No Fire. "Then if there's no chance of saving old Jeb, why did you all write that note to me and send it by an Indian runner?"

No Fire and Clint stared at each other, then both looked at No Fire's wife. Mutely, she shook her head.

"No one from here wrote anything to you, son," Clint said. "We . . . well, we talked some about letting you know, but I knew you was working hard out there, swinging things mostly by yourself, trying to build up a new ranch in strange country. We decided we just wouldn't bother you."

"Bother?" Boot's voice was impatient, almost curt. "After all the loyalty old Jeb Fentress has shown this ranch? Why, I'd ride through hell or high water to side him, to save him. That's exactly what I'll do if I have to!"

"But after he insists he did it? After he has already been sentenced to hang? Tice Bowman was shot in the back, evidently from pretty close range and no doubt from ambush, and when Jeb swore he did it, there just wasn't anything attorneys could do."

"What was Tice Bowman's business?"

"He was building up a fine horse ranch, down at the foot of Sulphur Springs, not far from the old freedmen settlement of Jacktown. He had somehow wrangled a long-term lease through the Cherokee National Council—some kind of political pull. There's a lot of that going on these days, if a man has a lot of cash."

"Does . . . is his daughter going on with the operation?"

No Fire shook his head. "I doubt it. She moved her things back to Fort Smith, or at least out on Massard Prairie, to kinfolks near there. A woman couldn't run a horse ranch in the Territory. Roughnecks would steal her blind."

For a time there was silence, interrupted only by the sounds of the sputtering fire and the ticking of the big Seth Thomas clock.

"All right, now," Boot said abruptly. "What's this about having all blinds drawn, meeting me with a gun, having the corrals padlocked—and who in the hell is putting up with a bunch of squatters building junker shacks on our land?"

Clint lifted his head, and Boot saw the flare of the old fighting spirit in his eyes. Yet it was a fleeting thing, replaced with a look of vague despondency.

"There's going to be a time, son, when all this land we've been paying to run cattle on will be allotted in severalty. Instead of controlling thousands of acres, we may have about 160 acres each."

Boot looked at him. "I've heard that business before. I heard it twenty years ago, when I was just a kid."

"I know. But this time it's coming," Clint said. "Oh, it may be several years yet, enough time for us to kind of get out of the red, move our cattle to western ranges. You see, there are too many people preaching that this Arkansas River bottomland is too rich for grazing purposes. Fort Smith is growing. Other towns, too. There'll come a time when all this land will be drained and farmed, row-cropped, or put to grain. I see the handwriting on the wall. I think even your grandpa knew it. He just gambled he could make a fortune in cattle before it happened. And if it hadn't been for the floods that wiped out whole herds, he would have made it, too."

"But these cleared patches now, these shanties . . ."

"They're intruders, Boot," No Fire said. "But some of them were displaced from places like Missouri, during Reconstruction and all. We haven't had the heart to put them out. To tell the truth, the War put the Cherokee country in a mess. You know that."

Boot's glance measured his brother. "But this ranch here wasn't once run like a fort."

No Fire stretched out his long legs, the firelight throwing the shadows of his boots long across the floor.

"We've been losing some beef to rustlers. And a night or two, some snipers took a shot at Pa while he was coming from the corrals. That was after Jeb killed Bowman."

Boot said emphatically, "I don't believe Jeb shot any man in the back. I know old Jeb would kill a man, all right, but he'd have to have good reason. And I know he would square off and match guns face to face with anyone. Wasn't his ability with a six-shooter one of the qualifications that got him his foreman job here?"

Clint nodded. "But these days, even if you catch a thief, you'd better be careful about gunplay. This new hanging judge will pronounce the sentence of death even if killing a man appears to us to be justified. Judge Parker is dead set on stopping the law of the gun in Indian Territory."

Boot smiled wryly. "I'm afraid he has a long, long way to go." He rose and stretched, realizing he was bone weary and sore all over after his fight with Mace. "I'm going in to see Jeb tomorrow. He'll tell me the truth about that killing, or I'll jerk his head through the bars and wring his neck. Because somebody wrote me to come back and help save Jeb. There's a little bit of a mystery there that makes me think someone knows a hell of a lot more than has been told in court, or by old Jeb himself—and another thought strikes me. I found old Jeb dead drunk in Coke Hill one night, the only time in my life I ever knew he was a drinking man. Why? What about things like that, that don't make sense? Do you reckon he temporarily went out of his mind?"

Clint rose also. "Jeb is as sane as anyone." Then he looked carefully at Boot. "Who did you tangle with, just before you rode in?"

"It's the same old story, Pa. Mace Bracken. He braced me while I was stopped at Ma's grave."

"You best him?"

"Did I ever fail?"

Clint looked into the firelight. "There may be a way of saving Mace, son. You know, the older I get, the more I understand. It's the old game of the have-nots against those that have. As the saying goes, those that have got, have got to lose. I don't think Mace actually hates you and No Fire as individuals. It's just because he grew up a snotty-nose kid, his folks Coke Hill derelicts, while you boys—"

"Pa!" Boot's voice was almost harsh. "Get away from that kind of thinking! I don't believe it! I've seen plenty of those Coke Hill boys go on to good jobs—at least jobs good enough to support families. Riding on the Choctaw horse ranches, cutting and hauling timber, working on the riverboats. And that about No Fire and me—why, you never handed us something for nothing. We worked for everything we had."

Clint was still staring moodily into the firelight when Boot said goodnight and sought his old familiar room across the hall.

He was weary in all his body, but sleep would not come at once. There was dread in this house, a feeling of impending disaster. He tried to shake the feeling, tried to concentrate upon his trip to see Jeb in the jail cell tomorrow, hoping he could do something to help the old man. But there was that feeling in the Hook Nine ranchhouse, weird as the whine of a wolf in fear. . . .

# Chapter Six

The sun was like a silvery ball of fire above the crest of the Arkansas as Boot rode down the slope of land between lines of stunted willows and halted Taw at the dock of the ferry that would carry them across to Fort Smith.

He saw that the ferry was on the opposite shore of the river, and he sat in his saddle quietly, just looking at the town.

Old Fort Smith—that was what the hard-drinking men of Indian Territory called the town, and with good reason. There was a saloon on every corner of the wide, dusty run of Garrison Street, and plenty more in between.

Above the Commercial Wharf stood a line of bawdy houses, some of which were as lavishly furnished as the bordellos he had seen in the notorious Storyville section of New Orleans during an adventurous riverboat trip one time.

He was aware that the ferry had started crossing slowly toward him, but he continued to look at the buildings at the far edge of the river, thinking that Fort Smith was really no worse, or much better than a hundred other places that were playing out their roles in the development of the West.

He frowned, remembering Pa's talk last night. It was difficult even for a man of foresight to believe that Old Fort Smith would eventually grow into a diversified city, and that the cattle and horse ranching domains of the Choctaw and Cherokee Nations might sometime fade away.

Boot watched a string of loaded freight wagons, two of them pulled by oxen, rolling down the slope from Garrison Street. His thoughts were torn between what he was seeing and the things he had sensed at the ranch early that morning as Pa and No Fire saddled up with the Hook Nine riders and took off toward Sulphur Springs Hollow and the timbered regions of Garrison Creek.

Bristling with guns, the outfit had been. No Fire and Pa had also been carrying weapons, which was a usual thing. But somehow the old free and easy spirit of the ranch had dwindled. Boot had sensed caution, and that puzzling web of tension that could be caused by nothing except the insidious tentacles of fear.

He heard the ferry ram against the plank side of the landing with a resounding bang. Taw snorted and reared, then pitched once high in the air before Boot heaved his head up. Half angered, Boot dismounted and forcibly led the spooked horse onto the ferry.

The gaunted ferryman, pale-faced, sick and bleary-eyed, had evidently been on an all-night binge.

Boot held Taw's reins tightly while the boat made the return trip. He looked upriver, where a riffle of faster water showed the mouth of the Poteau, the French-named stream that edged along the Choctaw–Arkansas line.

He was reluctant to let his glance stray toward the point where the squalid shanties stood, their makeshift roofs and porches tilted drunkenly. This was Cocaine Hill, and the blind tiger infested area of Smoky Row. It was the Old Choctaw Strip, a veritable no man's land between the Arkansas line and the deep, muddy cut of the Poteau. All the buildings were scattered topsy-turvy across land where a proud little frontier fort had once stood.

Nothing remained of even the second fort now except the unkempt, ivy-grown commissary building close to the river, the caving remains of the quartermaster's structure, and the old red brick barracks building that housed the chambers of Judge Isaac C. Parker's new "hell on the border" court.

Boot turned his gaze downriver. He saw a steamboat churning around Cherokee Bend. Beyond were the foothills of the Ozark, thirsting for water, the leaves of the trees already burned brown and sear. Sight of the mountains eased his thoughts of Cocaine Hill and the sordid-looking Jansen home where Ina lived.

He didn't want to think of Cocaine Hill or the barracks building and Judge Parker's infamous dungeon jail. Jeb Fentress was inside that stinking hellhole, already scheduled to hang.

"Hell," Boot muttered, shoving a growing dread from him. "I'm getting as bad as my brother and Pa."

The freight wagons and a couple of drummer's hacks stood waiting in line as the ferry touched the Fort Smith landing. The drivers of the freight wagons were probably headed for Fort Gibson or Tahlequah, Boot thought. They were uncommonly hard-eyed men, watching the shaky old ferryman suspiciously. The old man had not spoken one word to Boot, except for a shamefaced greeting, all the way across.

Boot paid his fare, led Taw off the boat, and mounted. He rode a short distance along Front Street, then reined up past the old commissary building and dismounted at the section of wall beside the Federal court.

Taw could be a cantankerous brute at times, but not one to desert his master. Boot left him with trailing reins in the shade of a maple and walked with a reaching and determined stride up the high steps and into the quarters for U.S. marshals.

Suddenly and unceremoniously, he found himself confronted by a burly deputy marshal who shoved the yawning bore of a pistol muzzle straight into his face.

"You crazy son!" the lawman gritted. "Don't you know better than to stomp in here with a six-shooter on your hip?"

Boot Lantry's first impulse was to slap the pistol aside and floor the man with a straight right against his mouth, but he saw the cylinder of the gun roll and heard the hammer snap back to full cock. Boot looked into the deputy marshal's eyes then, and their steely glint held him stilled.

"I've been in this place before. When Judge Story

had jurisdiction, I never had to check my gun."

"You do now! Turn around."

"That's stupid!" Boot flashed. "Get that gun out of my face! I'm not a criminal. I'll take off my gun, if you insist, but I won't be stripped down like a captured outlaw. My name's Lantry."

Boot's dark gaze, heated and steady, held the deputy marshal's eyes. He saw the change as the Lantry name registered, and pride of place and homeland surged through him like a flame in the Cherokee Hills.

"Lantry? All right. You'll still have to take off that pistol. Unbuckle your belt and hand it to me." The gun in the deputy marshal's hand stayed steady. "One wrong move, though, and you'll be dead. It was a crazy thing, barging in here armed."

Boot unbuckled his belt and handed it and the holstered pistol to the deputy marshal. The burly man took the gun and laid it on a desk against the wall. He then holstered his own weapon and gestured to a chair.

"Sit down."

"Thanks but I'm in a hurry," Lantry said. "I want to talk with Jeb Fentress."

The deputy marshal slowly took a chair in front of the desk, pulled a cigar from his vest pocket and lit it. He blew smoke toward the ceiling, his steely gaze measuring Boot.

"Talk, talk, talk," he murmured cynically. "That's all I've heard about that old killer, ever since we sacked him in. Lawyers in and out, somebody from the Lantry ranch, even a woman, pleading that the old son-of-a-gun is innocent. Don't you know that any kind of plea you make now won't do a bit of good?"

"Why won't it?"

"Why? Why, hell, Judge Parker has sentenced the man to be hanged by the neck until he's dead. Why can't you people understand that? The old man's as same as dead."

Boot stared at him intently. "There's always the chance of appeal."

The deputy marshal pushed back his straight-brimmed black hat and laughed. "That's a joke! Sure, you have the right of appeal, but do you know something? There is only one place where that appeal will go—to the desk of Judge Isaac Parker. And he's never reversed one of his decisions yet."

Boot felt the tension and unease flick through him and slowly dwindle away.

"Could I talk to Fentress now?"

The deputy marshal rose. "Sure. We won't deny you that privilege." For an instant there was sympathy in his gaze. "But there's one thing you fellows in the Indian Territory have got to learn. The day of gun law there is being wiped out. Killing, robbery, rape, thievery—we're stamping them out like rattlesnakes." The deputy paused and gestured. "That old gibbet outside is going to squeak and clang and necks are going to snap until—"

"You don't have any right to preach to me," Lantry snapped. "Save it. I've always been for law and order. I've also been firm in my convictions that a man needs gun protection over there across the line. Say I kill a man in self-defense—would you say that's a hanging offense?"

"Try it and see, Lantry. Just go out and try it and see. No man takes justice into his own hands over there now. Judge Parker has absolute and final jurisdiction over seventy-four thousand square miles of country that reaches all the way to the Colorado line. You try to take the law into your own hands now and kill a man, and you'll hang."

"I was talking about self-defense."

The deputy marshal turned to a peg on the wall and took down a ring of keys. "I'm not the judge, and like you say, I don't have any right to preach. I'm just telling an intelligent man what I know. I would venture to say that the only self-defense that will save your life now is to get on a horse and ride away from trouble fast—or if you aren't on a horse, you better start running like hell."

Lantry's laugh was curt, bitter. "I'd say you fellows are trying some hellacious kind of law enforcement around here now."

"It's the law of the Western District Court of Arkansas, with jurisdiction over all the Indian Nations. Judge Parker's law—not mine. Come on. I'm filling in while the jailer eats a late breakfast. I'll let you talk to Fentress now."

The deputy's big boots clumped heavily across the floor and down the outer steps. Boot followed, his footsteps light, quiet. The deputy turned left and went down a couple of steps to a high, steel-barred door in the barracks basement. A heavy outer wooden door stood ajar to let in air.

A rank odor of sweaty and filthy men struck Boot's nostrils. For an instant he froze, his gaze trying to pierce the darkness of the dungeon, trying to separate those constantly moving, restless human shapes inside.

"How many do you have penned up in there?" he asked tightly.

"About two hundred now. We'll have more next week . . . unless a dozen or so are hanged."

The barred door swung open under the deputy's big hands. He leaned in and called down the aisle between the twin rows of cells. "Fentress! Jeb Fentress! I'm allowing a visitor five minutes with you. Step out!"

A rush of wheezing breaths sounded, and the stench at the entrance was worse. Then Boot heard old Jeb's voice, the familiar, firm ring of it.

"I don't want to see anyone. I've told you that!"

Boot leaned in, his eyes adjusting to the dimness, and said quietly, "It's Boot Lantry, Jeb. I need to talk to you.'

There was a time of quietness except for the pulsating, uneven breathing of scores of prisoners and the occasional clang of shackles against concrete.

"All right, Boot," Jeb said. "I'll talk a minute. You know that. Come on in."

"Five minutes!" the deputy warned.

Boot passed him and moved down the dim corridor. One of his boots struck something, and he heard a slosh and smelled the rank stink of refuse or garbage. Fury almost choked him, but he quelled the urge to kick the can over and went on.

"Here, Boot," Jeb's voice said.

Boot stopped, and saw the shape of a hand thrusting between the bars of a cell.

He took the hand with a clamp of iron and felt the

strong response. He sensed again, as he had so many times, the strength in this man.

Then old Jeb's face became visible; it was not the face Boot remembered at all. Jeb Fentress had always been clean shaven in a land of bearded or moustached men. Now Jeb's face was covered by a heavy growth of beard. It made him almost a stranger, there beyond the iron bars, and the feeling was intensified as his hand pulled away from Boot's clasp.

"Jeb, we're going to get you out of here."

Jeb's voice was steady. "I don't see how."

"You didn't do it, Jeb. You didn't shoot a man in the back."

"Yep. Yep, I sure did, Boot. I shot him dead."

"In the back, Jeb? From behind, from ambush, without giving Bowman a chance?"

"You heard me. I let him have it. High in the back, high above his belt. He was dead before he hit the ground."

"Why, Jeb? Why would you do a thing like that?"

Fentress's face was going back from the bars, and he was a man unattainable, unreachable, leaving Boot.

"I'd been watching Bowman," Jeb's fading voice said. "I figured he had bad things in mind for your daddy's Hook Nine. Bad things, Boot. That's all I'll ever tell you. So long, now, son, and don't come back here. I won't see you. I don't want anyone worrying, or anything. Hell, I know I'm going to hang. It's just three days from now. But I'm not afraid to die."

"Jeb . . ."

But the old man was gone, pressing back out of sight in the mass of men, and suddenly a bearlike figure lunged against the bars and a man's insane voice shouted, "Let th' ol' bastard alone! Leave him! Let 'im step out and die with me. I'm dropping three days from now, too. He ain't got no right to live, if I ain't. Git on out of here!"

Boot turned slowly and walked down the dank corridor. He noticed that the deputy marshal's face looked tight and strained as he reached the door.

"You see what I meant about this talk, talk, talk. I don't want any more of it. You hear?"

Boot's face didn't change expression. "You may hear more of it. Is the judge in his chambers now?"

The marshal shut and locked the big steel door and wheeled around. "He's there. But any talk you have for him will be a waste of breath."

"We'll see."

Boot turned on into the sunlight, feeling the cool beat of the October wind and smelling the cleanness after the stench of the jail's interior. He was going ahead of the deputy marshal, back up the stairway of the Federal building, when the clatter of hoofbeats and jangle of harness trappings caused him to pause and face the street.

"Ah!" murmured the deputy. "More prisoners coming in."

It was hard to tell whether the ring of his voice carried satisfaction or a faint amazement. The mule-drawn wagon had halted, and the bearded driver was holding the lines tensely as two deputy marshals, holding shotguns, eased down from the springseat and straightened on the street.

Boot watched as they leaned over the sideboards of the wagon, punching the sprawled forms of three men with the shotgun muzzles.

The men came erect slowly, stiffly, handcuffed, their legs in chains. They were bare-headed, beardless, the collars of dirty shirts open. Long, stiff mops of black hair, tangled and matted, almost covered their eyes.

"Why, they're a bunch of kids!"

The words crackled from Boot's lips like pistol shots, echoing in the morning air.

"Yeah. Killer kids from the Choctaw Nation," the deputy said.

Boot watched with slitted eyes as the youths were hauled out of the wagon and hustled into the dungeon jail. The door clanged shut and the deputies waved the driver away.

They came up the steps toward Boot. His harsh voice challenged them. "What have those kids done?"

The deputy marshals stopped. They were three steps below Boot Lantry, and one of them looked exceptionally small. But it was easy to sense the strength in him, and the fiery nerve that would go up against all odds. His hat was set level and Boot saw the bullet holes in its crown. The man's head tilted up; Boot found himself looking into piercing, slate-gray eyes. He came up another step and offered his hand to Boot.

"I'm Travis Reaves. Who're you?"

"Boot Lantry." His glance locked with that of the deputy, and it was almost like the clash of sabers. "What did the youngsters do?"

"Just rape and murder. Four persons killed, that's all."

Boot jerked a thumb over his shoulder, gesturing across the Choctaw line. "They have tribal courts over there."

The deputy's gray eyes never flickered. "Sure. Do-nothing courts. The kind that turn murderers loose on their honor, and that big myth that the killers always return to hang. What's all this to you? What're you all stirred up about?"

Boot gestured beyond the gibbet, toward Cocaine Hill and Smoky Row.

"Why don't you marshals nab some of the killers right here in your own back yard?"

"Like who?"

"Like Mace Bracken, or Hemp Surate, or a half dozen or so more I could name!" Boot's voice went low, gruff with challenge and fury. "How do thugs like them manage to dodge you?"

The marshal said flatly, "If they ever overstep themselves, and we know it, they won't. I've heard no complaints. What did you say your name is, friend?"

"Boot Lantry."

A fleeting change of expression touched the wiry marshal's face. "I see. I remember. You had a gun brawl on the Row not too many years ago."

"Two years ago," Boot said.

"No one was killed in that one."

"No. But the young Dakin boys were framed and had to leave the country. I haven't heard from them since."

"I have."

"When?"

"Two weeks ago. They robbed a mail hack at

70

Verona. Marshals are after them now in the Cookson Hills.''

The deputy's glance dropped from Boot's level stare then, and he came on up the steps past Boot and entered the court building. Boot turned and followed him, shouldering through the doors of the entrance hall and rapping with his knuckles on the heavy paneled door of Judge Parker's chambers.

From beyond the door a deep voice asked, "Who is it, please?''

Boot identified himself and waited briefly, and when he was invited in he knew it was the rumbling deep voice of Fort Smith's "Hanging Judge.''

# Chapter Seven

There he was.

He was a big man, crowding forty, square built, wide and heavy in the shoulders and heavy of features. This heaviness was intensified by a drooping moustache that flowed around and down into a neatly trimmed goatee.

His hair was thick, buffed out behind and over his temples, and flowing to the left above his massive brow like a tufted cowlick, enhancing the brilliance of his piercing dark eyes.

Evidently he had already handled early court business. He was robed for the bench, standing near a cherrywood desk. Beyond him on the wall, reflecting his image, was a gilt-framed mirror. He was holding a Bible and some papers.

One of his hands barely moved, gesturing toward a chair. He switched the Bible and papers from one hand to the other, and took out a gold-plated watch and looked at it.

"I have three minutes until the next case, Mr. Lantry. What can I do for you?"

Boot had taken off his hat respectfully. He held it, his right hand softly stroking the crown. He answered without preliminaries. "You can review the case of Jeb Fentress and free him. He isn't a guilty man."

"Sit down, Mr. Lantry," Judge Parker said.

Boot Lantry quietly complied.

There was a time of stillness. It was so quiet in the chambers that Boot could hear the ticking of the judge's watch.

"Jeb Fentress will hang for murder at exactly ten o'clock Thursday morning, Mr. Lantry. If you care for a permit to witness the hanging, I shall have one issued to you."

The tone of finality in the judge's words made Boot immediately rise.

"You can't hang an innocent man!"

"I've never hanged any man!" the deep voice thundered. It's the law that hangs these men. I've made that clear to journalists. I don't have time today to explain all phases of justice to you."

Boot stood half in profile to the judge. He turned his eyes, letting their sideward impact take in Judge Parker from his feet to the top of his head.

"Three days is mighty short time for me to rake up any evidence that might save him," Boot said. "I've just returned from the Verdigris River. Your Honor, I'm pleading now for more time to find evidence that may save a friend. Jeb Fentress's plea of guilty sounds to me like that of a man temporarily out of his mind.

He had no reason to kill Tice Bowman. Even if he had, Jeb would have done the job fair, face to face, like—"

"Like the gun-fighting killer he is. I've repeated time and again, from the bench and at private gatherings, that the law of the gun shall no longer prevail in the Indian country. The crimes that are happening there are a disgrace to this nation and the world. It would pay you to take my words into account, Mr. Lantry. There shall be no more gun-law in the jurisdiction of my court."

Boot stood a moment, looking at the controversial figure, sensing the power vested in the man and feeling a vague despair at the formidable weight of it.

"Your Honor, you don't have enough deputy marshals to patrol all the Indian nations. If men out there—men like myself, and my brother and father— if we lay aside our guns, we're leaving our lives and our property fair game for anyone who wants to take them. Hasn't that ever occurred to you?"

"I've never insisted that any man travel through the country out there unarmed. I have taken into account everything involved in what the court has set out to do. And I know the things the court changes in that wicked land will not be changed in a day. I'm fully aware of many problems, Mr. Lantry. But those problems have nothing at all to do with Jeb Fentress. Not now. He admitted in fair trial before me that he was guilty of shooting a man in the back and killing him. The law says he must hang. Now, Mr. Lantry, our time is up."

He offered his hand. Boot took it. The judge's clasp was warm and firm.

75

Then he withdrew his hand and gestured toward the doorway, and Boot knew he was being dismissed.

Sunlight struck his eyes, and suddenly it was harsh and glaring, as harsh as this harsh street upon which he walked.

The voice of the judge was still thundering in his ears, forceful, inescapable. Boot reached Taw and mounted, and was moved by a sudden impulse to see and talk to Ina Jansen. There was a growth of frustration in him. He needed to see her, to hear her quiet voice.

Taw was eager for fast travel. The sound of his hoofbeats echoed against the walls of the commissary building as Boot reined him down the slope, past the crumbling fort walls and a riverfront store or two and on into the alleys that led between the shanties of Cocaine Hill.

Burlap sacks, used for summer awnings in front of some of the shanties, flapped in the riverside breeze. A tangle-haired floozie with a half filled wine bottle in her hand tottered up from a stool in the shade of a hackberry bush and shook the bottle tauntingly at Boot as he passed. Another woman, so thin her clothes merely hung on her, stared with the profound misery of someone sick drunk and constantly so: a female derelict beyond recall.

A few men snored on the floors of rotting porches. Two little tykes of boys rose from a sand pile and stared wide-eyed, not so much at Boot but at the sleek mount he rode.

Boot eased the black horse to a standstill and

turned in the saddle.

"You kids ever go up to Garrison Street, up where the big stores are?"

The little boys looked at each other. One of them lifted his chin belligerently. "We don't steal!"

"Good boys!" Boot took out his money pouch and crumpled a bill in his hand and tossed it to them. "Then don't let anyone steal from you. Take that, sort of quietlike, and slip off uptown and pay for and eat your fill of whatever you can find."

He winked as one of them stooped and snatched the bill off the ground. He sent Taw moving on.

The old Jansen shanty above the rugged stone Choctaw Wharf looked sorrier than ever, Boot thought, and the great cottonwood tree that had once arched branches over it apparently had been chopped down, possibly for winter firewood.

Boot halted his mount and stepped out of the saddle. He felt the wind from the river, damp and chilly against the back of his neck. There were no curtains at the windows, the way Ina had once kept them. He guessed she had taken them down to wash them. He might find her down at the river's edge, on the bluff where he had first met her, he thought. He started to turn that way, leaving Taw standing.

"Who you lookin' fer, mister?" a voice behind him asked.

Boot turned about. A toothless old man stood in the doorway, leaning heavily on a home-made walking stick.

"Ina Jansen," Boot said. "Miss Ina. Is she there in the house?"

"The Jansens don't live here now. Ain't lived here

77

for about a year or more. Not since Wes Cutler moved 'em out."

Down at the edge of the Choctaw Wharf the whip-crack of a rifle shot sounded. Someone shooting turtles for practice, Boot thought. The echoes from the shot formed a cushion of sound around his mind for an instant, helping to alleviate the shock of the old man's words.

"Cutler? Why would he move the Jansen family from here?"

"Well, ol' Tobe told me it was a likely sounding agreement. I think he and the family was gonna do some odd jobs and things, and get a good house free on the range Cutler leases from Indians."

The devilish truth of the matter was probing into Boot Lantry's brain. Ina Jansen's beauty was a part of that truth, but he doggedly tried to fight it down.

"Do you know what part of Cutler's range the Jansens moved to?"

The old man scratched his jaw. "Well, it ain't too fur. Ol' Tobe said so. Directly at th' foot of th' hills, I think, almost on the main road across the river there."

"Thanks."

Boot reached out to take Taw's reins, and felt the nervousness race down from his shoulders, running out through his hands. There was sudden sweat in his palm and a knot in his guts, and none of it eased until he hit the saddle. Then the surge of fury wiped out all tremors, and he was a tall man, quiet in the saddle, a deadly quietness, looking for a moment at the false fronts and the horses that were tied at the sagging hitch rails in front of the old Smoky Row saloons.

The thought was in him that he could use a drink, but he dropped it swiftly. A man with sense didn't drink when he needed a drink. No Lantry of the name ever had.

He turned Taw down toward the Choctaw Wharf, thinking he would take the rickety old Indian ferry across instead of the main ferry he had ridden earlier. He would land in the "Little Juarez" town of Moffett on the Cherokee side of the Arkansas and pick up the road to the Jansen place from there.

A thick-bodied Choctaw, naked from the waist up and wearing old army boots so big they turned high at the toes like the prow of a gunboat, rowed Boot and his horse across.

The far landing was as crude as the natural stone wharf at the mouth of the Poteau, only different: merely a bank of hoof-trampled sand, with a trail snaking off up the shore, past ramshackle dwellings and a scattering of illegal saloons and gambling houses that had given the place its nickname.

Boot looked at the sleepy run of the river and wondered briefly how many men had been murdered either at Moffett or Cocaine Hill and dumped into the drink betwen the sordid settlements. No one would ever know.

He was paying the Choctaw and fixing to lead Taw off the boat when he saw an Indian man on a spotted pony, his squaw perched up behind him, come trotting down the bank toward the ferry. The Indian was motioning imperiously for the Choctaw ferryman to wait.

A brief smile touched Boot's lips as he recognized the couple on the pony.

— "Hi, Indian Joe," he said. He touched his hat to Indian Joe's wife. "Good morning, ma'am."

"*Cee-oo*, Chooch!" Indian Joe said, but it was obvious that he was in a hurry. He touched something that swelled the left front pocket of his trousers, as if to conceal it. "We mak' trip to town," he added.

"That's a good-looking horse you have there, Joe. You riding for one of the ranchers now?"

"We have hundred dolla, too!" chirped Indian Joe's wife. Evidently she had been reading Boot Lantry's lips.

Indian Joe leaped from the pony and glared up at his fat wife. "Ol' woman," he growled, "sometime I beat hell out of you, you don't hush your mouth!"

She slid from the pony, her face stoical, looking quietly at her man. "You want good dip now, Joe?"

"No dip! No nothing! Ol' woman, you come on now!"

Indian Joe caught her arm with one hand and the reins of the spotted pony with the other. They boarded the ferry and the craft pulled slowly away from the shore.

Boot stood briefly, looking at the good spotted pony, wondering where Indian Joe had got the horse. Then, spurred by the thought that was roweling through his mind with such a cutting impact, he mounted and sent Taw at a long lope up the bank, past the shacks of Moffett and on out to the Tahlequah–Fort Smith road which he had traveled the day before.

The miles swept past, and Taw was still loping freely. The Sixkiller graveyard came into view, but Lantry merely glanced at it and kept riding, his gaze turning ahead and holding, framing a hill beyond Garrison Creek where a cabin with a full-length front porch stood.

He saw a faint plume of smoke welling up from a rusty stovepipe, and he visualized Ina Jansen, her pretty face flushed over a hot stove, preparing the noon meal. It was a picture that was alive in his mind because he had visualized it often while sitting around lonely night camps, far up the Verdigris.

But this time, the picture was very short-lived.

It was Taw that scented and sighted the cattle herd first; he was a natural-born cow-horse, and a calf or longhorn steer a mile away could put him on the alert.

The next instant Boot saw the cattle, a close-packed herd shuffling down from the foothills, pushed by a half dozen riders. The cattle reached Garrison Creek and spread out on a shoal, sniffing the rocks and bawling for water. Lantry stopped Taw and watched.

The riders were not whooping or making much sound at all, but they were crowding the cattle, turning them up the creek, winding them in and out along the staggered stream toward a place where Lantry knew there was a long pool, clean enough to wade in and cool enough to drink—water under Lantry lease.

At that instant Lantry recognized Wes Cutler, riding a high-headed red gelding with coppery mane and tail. Cutler was not giving any verbal commands, but his hands kept motioning urgently, slicing the air for emphasis as he placed riders here and there.

Boot Lantry touched Taw's neck with the reins and the big black spun and lunged off the road, crashing through the canebrakes and the alder thickets. Boot ducked as the low-hung branches of a hickory tree confronted him, then straightened, his gaze lining out to a point on the creek where he knew he could intercept the herd.

Taw took a matting of vines and creepers like a well-trained jumper, and his iron-shod hoofs slammed down into a nest of jumbled stones. The creek was there. Taw was halting and Lantry was reining him around, facing the first old mossy-horn bulls that rounded the bend.

"Turn 'em, Taw!" Boot said.

What happened next was mostly in the lightning-swift brain and brawn of the big cow-horse, because Lantry had little to do with the chore except to concentrate upon staying mounted.

Taw bolted toward the lead bull like something shot out of a gun. The bull snorted and spooked and tried to twist around inside his skin. One of his long horns slashed hide from the ribs of a steer as he twisted, and the steer bawled and twisted too.

Then Taw went to the left, lunging into the herd and out of it, stirring up a sudden and frantic milling that turned into a stampede of the leading cattle, back toward those in the rear.

The exuberance and fast action of the horse got to Boot Lantry, making the blood pound in his throat and temples. As Taw wheeled and charged back to the right, almost slamming against the stragglers on that side, Boot drew his pistol and tilted the muzzle upward, firing into the elements.

Before the echoes of the shot had finished their tapping off through the tree trunks, the entire herd was doubling back. The lead bulls were streaking through the timber north of the creek, plunging past Cutler and his yelling riders with such abandon that nothing could stop them, not even the shuddering trees and saplings against which their shoulders and bellies slammed.

It was only then that Boot put pressure on Taw's bridle reins, finally drawing the big horse in. He holstered his pistol and leaned forward, running his fingers through Taw's mane, fondly slapping the big horse's neck.

"You're some hoss, Taw!" Boot said.

The herd was gone, and the sound it made back up the mountain was now like dwindling thunder, distant and remote, as if the cattle only moments ago had taken no part in or headed no portion of the present scene on Garrison Creek:

A confrontation. . . .

# Chapter Eight

A lone man on a huge black horse, facing six glowering riders; young and brash and angered young men with pistols belted to their thin bellies, slightly fronted by an older man—Wes Cutler—who was carrying a concealed weapon, if any at all, but whose eyes were spilling murder.

"Lantry!" Cutler said as recognition dawned on him. He was holding himself, holding, holding. Boot could tell it, could witness it, weigh it and judge it. "Lantry, what in the name of creation does this mean?"

"You know what it means!"

"I don't. I'll swear I don't." He writhed in his saddle, looking at his riders, then back to Boot, and his stance was like that of a man tiptoeing on the verge of a precipice, almost impelled to leap, but dreading that deadly fall.

And Boot sensed where the real fear lay. He saw

Cutler's glance sweeping past him and around him, and Boot knew that Wes Cutler was not certain that Boot Lantry was alone. Cutler had no way of knowing that there were not some hidden Hook Nine men, crouched behind Boot in the underbrush, guns at the ready, waiting for Cutler or his riders to make one false move.

Cutler spread his hands in a gesture of helplessness.

"Explain to me, Lantry. Why did you stampede my cattle?" His eyes bulged, showing rings of wrathful, bloodshot whiteness around the portions that held his sight. "Those were my cattle—are my cattle! I was taking them to the new range I leased."

"There's no range along this creek that you can lease, Cutler. Not one grassy, or brushy, or rocky acre of it. You're on Lantry range."

"But this Indian—this fellow called Joe. He . . ." Cutler fumbled for papers in a small folder in the pocket inside his coat. "Joe signed a lease. Said he owns this land, that his cousin is chief."

Cutler's voice dwindled away as Boot Lantry laughed.

"Indian Joe has sold rights to this creek land to a dozen takers. None of the takers ever got to stay. A smart Indian, that Joe."

"If my lease won't stick, how can yours?" Cutler demanded.

"Mostly because we beat you, Cutler. We beat you by several years. And that's not all. We own this land in common with hundreds of other Cherokees."

"You don't look Indian to me!"

"I'm Indian enough."

86

The five young riders were easing their horses forward, their glances darting at Cutler, then at Boot. In another instant Cutler would give them the signal, Boot knew. Wes Cutler couldn't hold his fury all day. That was plain.

The seconds were ticking out into an eternity and Boot was tensing for a bloody shoot-out, when his gaze caught a flash of color, moving swiftly through the bushes on the north bank of the stream.

He saw the blond hair then, and the face of Ina Jansen. She was hurrying past the riders, coming into full view, sliding down the creek bank, stumbling, straightening, walking with wide, cornered eyes toward Boot Lantry.

There was going to be a sudden burst of gunplay and Ina Jansen was walking straight into the line of fire.

There was no time for Boot Lantry to look at Ina and reflect on his dreams of her.

"Ina, don't come close to me!"

He was looking at Wes Cutler as he said it, not at her. But he was conscious that she had not slowed, that she was still crossing the rocks of the creek toward him.

"Ina!" Boot's voice was low, but freighted with relentless command. "Get back!"

Evidently the impact of his command stopped her. Boot knew it as he saw Cutler's glance flash sideward in her direction and hold still.

The sideward movement of Cutler's eyes was the thing that ripped out of his ruthless hands a portion of the overwhelming power he held here. When he pulled his glance away from Ina Jansen, he was looking into the muzzle of Boot Lantry's gun.

Fear of death suddenly made Cutler's face look flaccid. His blue-tinged lips opened, sucking in one swift breath.

"Lantry, don't . . ." he started to say, then the fury that mingled with his fear made him catch it. His bulging orbs cut around again, throwing his glance over the faces of his riders.

They were sitting still and straight in their saddles, but it was an explosive stillness. Cutler's eyes reflected knowledge of that, the certain knowledge that his young riders would side him.

"Lantry, you're a fool to think you can best us here."

The pupils of Boot Lantry's eyes glittered cold between his thick, black lashes. He had thumbed back the hammer of his heavy Colt, and the muzzle of the pistol was centered on Cutler's heart.

Boot didn't say anything. He didn't feel there was any need.

"You men stop this—this awful thing!" Ina Jansen cried. The sound of her voice echoed up and down the creek and against the northerly foothills, but no one looked at her or paid any heed.

"A fool," Cutler repeated, but his voice lacked conviction. His eyes dilated as he looked at the gun in Lantry's hand, then he shot a fast look at his riders, his right hand lifted slightly. Boot saw that it was shaking. "No, boys! No! Don't do anything rash."

"Hell," one of the young riders said, contemptuously and unfeelingly. "You think one gun can outdo this crowd?"

Cutler writhed in his saddle again. "I know it,

boys! He couldn't! But . . ."

"But I can take you before I go, Cutler. You know that, too."

Boot's voice was soft, unemotional, but it made Wes Cutler flinch. He rose in his saddle and spat, fast, three times in succession, as if he had swallowed a spider and was rankly resentful of it.

"We'll . . . we'll let you off this time, Lantry. We'll let you off." Cutler's shoulders sagged briefly, then he squared up and looked at Ina, then back to Boot. "But I'm warning you and all your clan to stay out of my business from now on."

Boot didn't answer him.

"Completely out of my business," Cutler insisted. "Do you hear that? Completely! Ina and I will be married soon. We'll go East for a few weeks, but we'll establish our home here. If you ever attempt to bother us in any way, my men will cut you down."

Boot's tongue felt dry and thick, but he managed to get the words out. "I'll hear it from her, Cutler. Move out!"

He shoved his pistol about three more inches forward. There was an urge in him to squeeze the trigger, to be rid of Cutler for good. It was riding Boot like a spectre, and Cutler must have instantly sensed it.

He made a small gagging sound and wheeled his horse, motioning a limp-looking left hand for his riders to follow him. They turned their horses reluctantly, still watching Boot, then their mounts matched the speed of Cutler's gelding. They disappeared in the woods.

Boot listened while the crackle of hoofbeats faded

up the mountain slope, then he holstered his gun and dismounted. The stones of the creekbed felt hard under his bootheels. He didn't want to look at Ina at once.

He wanted that killing fury to fade from his eyes before he looked at her.

"Boot," she said. "I want to talk to you."

Her voice had the same soft, remembered impact, and that was strange, he thought, in the face of what he had heard Cutler say. He knew he had to absorb the shock of Cutler's words and face her squarely. He did it, walking to meet her, taking off his hat.

"It's good to see you, Ina," he said. He waited, wondering if she would offer her hand, but she didn't.

But she stood close to him, a slender girl with finely drawn features crowned by blond hair that was combed back a bit too severely and twirled into a roll at her neck. Her hands were restless, touching her hair, smoothing her dress, swiftly fingering her cheeks and brow.

Her gaze was steady, but there was none of the warmth he had expected of her.

"Talk is already running wild here, Boot," she said. "I don't like to hear it."

"What kind of talk, Ina?"

"Oh, Papa tells me what people are saying. Papa's beginning to tell me many things. He says people are saying you'll kill Mr. Cutler. That you'll cause trouble here, just like . . ."

"I may do that very thing."

Usually her eyes were mild, but suddenly he saw that fire in them.

90

"Boot, you can be a loser for once. I know how you and your father and brother never could stand to lose anything, not even a beef that someone took to feed his family, but—"

"We gave away lots of beef, Ina. We always did that, to the needy folks that asked us—and even to the needy that never asked, if we happened to know."

"But there were so many times when you never knew!"

Boot said calmly, "We tried to keep in touch with the needy, but we balked when it involved meddling with another man's affairs."

"Yes, but the way you hounded people when they stole a calf or something."

"I hate a thief. I hate a thief worse than a rattlesnake. I have more respect for a man that comes up with a gun and takes something. I always did."

But Ina Jansen was set for dissension, for argument with him. She made it plain.

"And the Lantrys never would lend money to folks," she said. "Never!"

"That isn't true."

"I know it is! I knew some fellows once from Cocaine Hill, and they tried to borrow money from your father for a trip to New Orleans. They needed to get down there to find jobs, but—"

"Those thugs weren't looking for jobs," Boot interrupted. "Pa offered them work, and they wouldn't take it. But they sure tried to raise a stink against us, just because we wouldn't lend them money for a high-faluting trip to the big town. There's a difference between lending money to someone who needs it, and just handing out money to fill somebody's whims. You know that."

"But your folks always had plenty of money," Ina said.

Boot looked at her. "It doesn't make any difference if a man's a millionaire, he doesn't owe it to anyone to dole out money just to satisfy a neighbor's desire. I know how some people claim the Lantrys have been too lucky. But I've learned that the harder a man works, the luckier he gets. You see?"

Boot knew that their talk was running on tangents, dodging around the real issue that was filling their minds. But squarely up against the stark truth that things between him and Ina Jansen had come to such a plight.

Then suddenly, because he was what he was, he accepted the fact that it was futile to dodge. Resentment tinged his face with deeper color. He said with a low and brittle scorn, "I guess Wes Cutler is free with his money. Doling it out so the Jansens can take life easy. Isn't that about the way it is?"

"No, that isn't the way it is!" she retaliated. "It's like Mr. Cutler said. We're going to get married and spend a few weeks in the East. But we're coming back here to live, and we're going to live in peace, do you hear me? You're not going to insult decent people just because you're a Lantry, just because you have power and land rights. You're going to leave us alone, do you hear?"

Boot struggled against the growth of sickness in him. "Ina," he said quietly. "What happened to you?"

"Nothing happened to me. It happened to you. You can't blame me for wanting to get away from

Cocaine Hill, for wanting a better house to live in. And you can't blame me for accepting Mr. Cutler's proposal of marriage. You could have stayed at home, Boot, and we could have built a life together. But, no, you had to strike out on your own, all the way out into wild country where I would never agree to live. Anything that has happened is all your fault."

"You're acting on impulse, Ina," Boot said. "I think it's because somehow I hurt you. If I did, I'm sorry. We could see each other again. We could talk this out."

She wrung her hands. "Boot, you're so violent! You always seem to be in trouble, even siding with outlaws like the Dakin boys. That was a terrible thing."

"The Dakin boys were being framed for cattle stealing, when I knew the stealing was being done by Hemp Surate, that Smoky Row barkeep and restaurant operator. Hemp needed beef for his restaurant business, and maybe other business, too."

"But the way you always pack a gun . . ."

"I'm pretty sure Wes Cutler carries a weapon, hidden under his coat."

"Yes, but he carries a gun because he has to," Ina defended. "Because people are always so ready to jump him. Oh, he's an ambitious man, Boot! He wants a position in affairs, so he can help people better themselves here. He told me so. And I warn you, Boot, I'll never speak to you, never even look at you again if you keep trying to block his way."

"Then you will see me again, Ina? We can talk?"

Her fingers touched her hair, and he saw that they

93

were trembling. "Well, Boot, I don't think so. I . . ."

"Think about it, Ina. Just think about the way things used to be between us. I'll give you time. And I won't step in Cutler's way, won't block his interests, as long as he keeps his cattle off Lantry range."

"Is that a promise, Boot?"

"It's a promise. You take time to think things over now." He turned from her and was taking up Taw's reins when another thought hit him. "And thanks for sending the message, Ina."

He stepped to the saddle, and took time to judge the blank look on her face.

"What message, Boot?"

"About old Jeb Fentress. How he was accused of killing a man. About him being sentenced to hang."

"Why, I haven't heard anything about someone being killed, or about Mr. Fentress."

Lantry's eyes narrowed. "You mean you haven't heard about Tice Bowman being killed? About the marshals arresting our foreman for murder? I thought you said your father told you things."

"He didn't tell me that. Never—and I've stayed close to home, canning garden stuff this summer. No one else had the chance to tell me anything. I haven't seen anyone."

"You've seen Wes Cutler. Didn't he ever say anything?"

Ina flushed, and the restlessness intensified in her hands. "Mr. Cutler is a gentleman. He told me once he didn't want me to be troubled by unpleasant things. He . . ." She stopped. Her eyes got round and brilliant. "Why, that must have been what my brother Sully meant, that day you came back home!

94

Sully said he thought he knew the reason you were riding so fast. Was that the reason you came home, Boot? Because of Jeb Fentress I mean?"

"That's the main reason, Ina. Goodbye now."

He touched Taw's neck with the reins and the big horse wheeled and leaped up the bank of the creek. Boot rode without looking back.

# Chapter Nine

There was no desire in him to ride back to town, or to the ranch. He wanted to be alone. He wanted to ride slowly, up through the timbered canyons that pushed back into the rugged foothills. He wanted to think.

He circled wide from the creek, holding Taw to a walk through a flat, parklike area scant of underbrush but abundant with tall gum trees. Taw's hoofs sank deep in the rich, loamy soil, and Boot thought again of what his father said.

"There'll come a time when this land will be drained and farmed, row-cropped or put to grain."

It wasn't something Boot Lantry wanted to see. He had seen the farms along the lower Arkansas and along the Mississippi, on that trip to New Orleans. He had seen men walking in plowed furrows, sweating and holding to the handles of mule-drawn plows. He had seen first-hand grueling back labor and the confinement of fenced acres. It wasn't a picture he liked to recall.

He thought of the Verdigris country, remembering the open meadows, the sweep of prairie, the hundreds of miles of unfenced grass waving in the breeze.

But he doubted that Ina would ever side him in that country he was beginning to love, and that thought made his love for the prairies dwindle somewhat. It was a hurting thing, this problem about Wes Cutler and Ina Jansen. It could cut a man to the quick.

He circled Taw, coming again to Garrison Creek, crossing it and following its twisting course into the higher hills.

He got his first look at the Bowman Circle S Ranch on a point of land below Sulphur Springs Hollow. It was a large house with a circular porch and dormer windows, overlooking a massive stable complex and rows of cedar log corrals. It was a place of rare beauty in this wild land, Boot thought. He saw several wranglers about, working with the tall, sleek Tennessee walkers. Beyond the house, winding up Garrison Creek, was the old military route, or one prong of it, that had been built from Fort Smith toward Tahlequah and Fort Gibson in 1826. This prong of the road led past the old Bellefonte Indian settlement, and the community of Verona near Little Lee Creek.

Boot's face altered when he thought of Verona. The Dakin boys, Lute and Stafford, had robbed a mail hack there, the marshal had said.

It was a difficult thing to believe. Boot had always

thought that Old Jim Bill Dakin's boys were honest. Lute and Stafford had sided Boot and No Fire in many boyhood adventures along Garrison Creek and up and down the Arkansas.

Still, if a girl he had loved and trusted could change so drastically, so could fellows like Lute and Stafford, he thought.

Boot was riding past the lower end of Dead Man's Hollow, his mind deep in thought, when Taw's lifting head and pointing ears alerted him. Boot halted the black and sat still in the saddle. On the road ahead he heard the jog-trotting sound of an approaching horse.

Boot reined from the road and halted behind a tangle of dusty grapevines. He was in no mood to meet anyone. He wanted neither company nor talk.

Or thought he didn't, until he recognized the huge, stoop-shouldered and gray-bearded man on the rangy dun.

Boot sent Taw at a slow walk from behind the grapevines.

"Jim Bill! How are you, man?"

Old Jim Bill stopped his mount as if the animal was about to wham up against a tree or rock wall. Instinctively, old Jim Bill Dakin's right hand dropped toward the butt of his low-slung gun.

Then he recognized Boot and his lips spread as his eyes crinkled in a happy smile.

"Boot Lantry! Think of the devil, and he'll sure appear! I was just thinkin' about you, Boot."

Dakin rode up close and offered his hand. They shook, smiling into each other's face, then by unspoken but mutual agreement, reined into the

99

shade to talk.

"Yes, sir, I was just thinkin' about you, Boot. Thinkin' how bad my two boys need a friend or two with influence. They're in one hell of a bind."

"Did they pull off that robbery, Jim Bill?"

"I don't think so. As far as I know, they haven't been out of Dead Man's Hollow for about two months. I've been bringin' 'em food. I reckon I need your advice more than anything else, Boot. Lute and Stafford want to give themselves up."

"No!" Boot said violently. He was thinking of that dungeon jail, the packed, sweaty human bodies, the unbearable stench. He wouldn't subject his friends to that. "Hell no!"

Old Jim Bill Dakin looked puzzled. "That ain't the answer I expected from you, Boot."

"No. I don't suppose it is. It isn't the answer I would have given, either, a few months or years ago. But it's the answer I'm giving now. If the federal jail at Fort Smith was decent, and if I didn't think the judge there is a fanatic, I'd say bring them in and let them take their chances. But my advice now, if the boys aren't guilty, is to have them head west—far west—and get some good honest riding jobs."

"It won't be easy. Lawmen are watchin' every trail an' byroad. The boys would have been captured long ago if they had really been in th' Cookson Hills, like th' marshals think. I figured they'd be safer right here, almost under Judge Parker's nose."

"That could be true, unless someone follows you to their hideout. You're taking a lot of chances, Jim Bill."

"Yeah. Yeah, I sure am. Boot, I'm . . ."

"What?"

"I'm not certain my boys are innocent of every-thing. It's a feelin' I have, like maybe they're lyin' to me."

"What causes that feeling, Jim Bill?"

"Well, I think it's that whelp of a Sully Jansen, ol' Tobe Jansen's boy. I found him squallin' drunk on white lightnin' whisky, down in th' woods yonder one day, and he swore he knows where Lute and Stafford are. Later, after he sobered, I tried to wring the truth out of him, but he wouldn't speak one word. But he sure put that feelin' in me."

Boot looked at the old man narrowly. "Sully was a personable kid when I left here, two years ago."

"Well, he ain't now," Jim Bill said. "He's just like his name, all sulled up and mean. He keeps a big pistol hid out and comes into th' woods to strap it on and do some shootin' practice, ever' chance he gets. He's turnin' out to be plumb bad. And nowadays, th' young ones like him are about th' worst."

Boot reflected on that, thinking of the young part-Indian prisoners the deputy marshals had brought to jail. Boot reined Taw around.

"I'll ride as far as the ranch turnoff with you, Jim Bill."

"No! Not on your life! You keep on up this road for a mile or so. I'll ride on by myself. I don't want to take the chance of getting you involved. I'll meet you in town later on and we'll talk some more. Maybe in a day or two. I do odd jobs, loading freight, some swamping in th' saloons, things like that. I'll see you around."

"All right, Jim Bill," Lantry said, and watched the

old man ride the dun horse along the dim road, around another bend and out of sight.

He had barely vanished when Boot heard the crack of an unshod hoof on stone high on the timbered ridge to the west. A loose range horse, he thought, but he pulled Taw behind the screen of vines again and waited. While he waited he drew his gun and carefully checked its mechanism. He broke out the cylinder and put back in the single load he had fired in the face of the Cutler herd.

The horse was coming slowly down the mountainside, a few steps at a time, stopping, then easing on. Boot traced snorting. He guessed the horse was grabbing a mouthful of mountain grass now and then. Boot was almost certain the horse was riderless. Hard as he tried, he couldn't hear any rattle of bit chain or squeak of dry saddle leather.

An outside horse, loose, unshod, just browsing along free and easy, Boot thought.

But it wasn't. The horse appeared through a dense cedar thicket, and there was a rider on it. The rider was hatless, coatless, bent forward to duck the limbs. It wasn't until he lifted his head that Boot recognized him, and even then it wasn't a swift thing.

Sully Jansen had grown considerably during the past two years. He was riding bareback, guiding his pony with an old rope hackamore. He was close and looming up big when he saw Boot. He jerked the pony to a halt abruptly and stared.

"Howdy, Sully," Boot said. He glanced up the steep pitch of the mountain. "You grabbed a rough route to ride on, didn't you, kid?"

"I'm not a kid! And I ride where I damned well please!"

Boot's gaze centered appraisingly upon him. "Well, Sully, I reckon I'm not challenging that. It was just a friendly remark I made."

"You can keep your remarks to yourself. I'm not the dumb kid everyone used to take me for. Not any more!" Sully said.

"I never thought you were dumb, Sully. I never said it, and never heard anyone else express the thought. It's all just in your mind."

"Like hell it is!" Sully rode closer. "Did you see a rider pass down here? Anyone ridin' along this road?"

Boot didn't answer that. He stared at Sully and thought how strange it was that a kid of his age should be wearing such a monstrous gunbelt and heavy pistol. His middle was freighted with belt, cartridges, tooled leather scabbard and gun.

"Where did you get that pistol, Sully?"

Sully Jansen laughed. "That's for me to know and you to find out," he said. He rode tauntingly closer, leaning sideward, letting the butt of the gun thrust up. "Take a good close look."

"All right."

Boot's right heel touched Taw and the big horse writhed sideward, slamming against the pony upon which Sully sat. Boot's left arm raked out, hauling Sully against him. At the same instant his right hand grabbed Sully's gun.

"I hated to do that, Sully. It was just to show you that when a man totes a pistol, he shouldn't go around daring someone to take it off of him. A man should have more respect for a gun than to just barge up and stick it out free for any hand."

He released Sully, letting him straddle back on his

103

pony. Then, because he didn't want to see the tears of rage in Sully's eyes, Boot sat Taw, quietly admiring the gun.

"It's a pretty good one, Sully. A .38 Special on a .45 frame. It sure is." Boot handed the gun back to him.

At the same instant, Boot drew his own. A man could never tell.

"Yep, you have a pretty fair gun there, Sully. It doesn't have the wallop and range of a .45 Colt like this, but it's still a pretty fair gun. Put it in the holster, now, and take good care of it."

Sully's belly was drawn in, and he was shaking like a leaf in the wind with rage and shame.

"I oughta kill you for that!" Sully whispered.

"Kill me, Sully? Just because I taught you a lesson that you ought to remember all your years?" Boot's cold glance thrust against him. "A real man handles a gun and packs a gun with respect, Sully. It's the wet-eared kids—the kind that fill early graves—that go around showing off. I wouldn't want you to die too young, Sully. I always thought you were a pretty good kid."

Sully cursed and spun his pony about, slashed its rump with the frayed rope reins and streaked away at a hard run in the direction of Old Fort Smith.

Boot followed, but at a slow pace, knowing Sully had already put almost a mile of distance between them and that several more miles would lie between them before the turnoff at the old ranch road.

Sundown was giving way to a rushing, silent

darkness when he again crossed the lower bend in the creek. He turned right on the winding old wagon road that led from the low creek meadows directly to the ranchyard gate.

He saw lights at the ranchhouse now, and he stopped a moment, reveling at the picture they made and thinking that maybe Pa and No Fire had gotten over their strange unease. He rode on then, past corrals and sheds, and stopped at the barnlot gate.

Dogs clamored a moment, but were silenced by a yell from the ranchhouse porch. Boot dismounted, opened the barnlot gate and led Taw through. He unsaddled and turned the horse free in the nearby pasture, then strode up the walk to the house.

He halted suddenly at the edge of the porch, seeing the shadows of silent people. There were too many people, riders for Hook Nine, standing bare-headed and quiet on the porch.

Puzzled, uneasy, Boot stepped forward, and they parted to make an aisle for him. Many candles were lit, illuminating the front room of the ranchhouse.

Boot stopped. He saw the two bodies, lying covered with separate sheets on the front room floor.

He looked across them, and saw Lawana, standing rigidly, her arms crossed tightly over her breasts. Her dark Indian eyes were deep pools of shock and grief.

Boot stopped, lifting the twin sheets one by one and lowering them. When he straightened, the front of his shirt was trembling with the pounding of his heart.

He was a Lantry alone. No Fire and Pa were dead.

# Chapter Ten

Two U. S. marshals followed by an ambulance wagon from the Napier Funeral Parlor arrived at the ranch before midnight. Boot turned the ambulance wagon back.

"Their coffins will be made here at the ranch," he told the driver. "Services will be held at the graveyard. That's our custom here."

The wagon driver sat a while in embarrassment. "Well, Mace Bracken told me Jeb Fentress has made good arrangements with us, because he's going to hang in a couple of days, you know. Mace said he figured maybe the Lantry family would also want the services of major undertakers."

"When did Mace Bracken learn about what happened here?"

The wagon driver shook his head. "Mace didn't tell me. But these days, we keep in close touch with the U. S. marshal's office at Fort Smith. I guess Mace got the news from there."

The driver glanced at the quiet-faced marshals, then straightened on the seat and clucked to the horses. The funeral wagon jolted through the darkness, empty, back toward Fort Smith.

Sloan Vestal, the Hook Nine subforeman, was the nearest to an actual witness that Boot Lantry could point out.

Boot had heard the story before, but he listened again, fighting his grief and shock with a dogged will.

"Old Clint was already dead when I got to him," Vestal told the marshals. "He was leaning back against the planks of the barnlot fence. But No Fire was still alive, and he had time to tell me he saw at least three mounted men. He said they were running their horses away from that stretch of woods up yonder."

"Was it still daylight? Plenty of light for him to count mounted men?"

"Yes. The rifle shots broke out just after sundown, while me and the crew was turning our horses out to grass in the pasture beind the barn. We had just rode in, and we would have all been out in front of the barn together, I guess, except I knew old Clint was tired. So I told some of the boys to take his horse, and the horse No Fire had been riding, too. We had just gone out of sight around the barn when the firing started. One thing No Fire told me before he died sure sticks in my mind. He said two of them riders looked like kids, maybe not more than sixteen or seventeen years old."

The marshals left the house and walked up to the

108

clump of woodlands, carrying a lantern to give them light, and tramped around for a while. They returned, measuring off the distance with even steps.

"We could have the bullets dug out, Lantry," one of them told Boot. "But I can't see much need of it. It was done with high-powered rifles, no doubt of that."

Boot nodded curtly. "The distance makes that plain. But thanks for coming out."

It was dismissal, but the marshals were having no part of it yet.

"Lantry."

Boot's face lifted. He stared at them.

"We know how you feel, but it's no time to be organizing private posses," one of the marshals said. "By daylight tomorrow, we'll have twenty deputy marshals combing the hills. We ought to have those killers hemmed in and captured in a few hours, just as soon as it's daylight and some tracking can be done."

"I hope you do," Boot said. That was all he said. The two U. S. marshals finally mounted their horses and rode away.

It was a quiet wake, with Boot and the Hook Nine men sitting without talking along the edge of the ranchhouse porch. The candles burned out before daylight, and Lawana, dry-eyed and beginning to get hold of herself, helped Boot fire up new ones.

Lawana had been kneeling beside a bed in the room she and No Fire had shared, drenching the sheet and mattress with tears almost all night long, but now she had cried herself out.

Sloan Vestal rode to Fort Smith and ordered new pine lumber and bolts of velvet. The material was delivered to the ranch by wagon when the sun was barely two hours high. Boot sat with Lawana, beside the sheet-covered bodies of Pa and No Fire, the sound of hammers and saws ringing in his ears. A direct man by nature, he asked Lawana, "What do you plan to do?"

"I'll go back to my people," she said.

"Sloan Vestal's a good man, and the riders under him are dependable, Lawana. Those fellows would protect you, if you want to stay here. The ranch and cattle are yours."

"No." Boot looked at her. "There's a young one on the way. No Fire's heir. And my property's on the Verdigris. I'll go back there as soon as the killers are found."

Lawana was a person of education. She had attended the Cherokee Female Seminary at Tahlequah. She thought about it for a while, then expressed her decision. "I'll accept half the price of the cattle, if you sell them. I think your father was something of a prophet. The time of big ranches will soon end here."

Lantry rose. He glanced across the two sheeted figures. Too many things ended too soon, he thought. He stood an instant, clenching and un-clenching his hands. He thought of Ina Jansen, of the parting of their ways; and mingled with thoughts of her were thoughts of the killers. His mind was bitter and grimly vengeance-bent.

He walked to the porch and looked across the wide sweep of the valley. He saw the smoky-green expanse of willows that marked the lowlands of Grassy Lake. His family had built an empire here that would soon

110

be gone.

Movement on the Fort Smith road caught his attention. It was a small, iron-gray horse pulling a topless buggy. He recognized Sue Bowman on the seat.

She pulled up at the front yard gate and stepped lightly down. She was hatless, her black hair wind-tossed and slightly disarranged. Boot noticed for the first time that she was a rather large girl, compared to Ina Jansen. She was wearing a gingham dress of light and dark blue plaid. She approached Boot and offered her hand.

"I'm sorry about everything, Mr. Lantry. I came as soon as I heard."

Boot looked at her, thinking of the unpredictable ways of womanhood. "Thanks," he said. Lawana came to the door and he introduced them, then Sue Bowman looked across the yard at the ranch crew.

"Mr. Lantry," she asked, "may I help the men?"

"Of course, if you want to."

She walked across the yard to the two pine coffins. She took the roll of velvet and a pair of scissors and went to work.

Pa and No Fire lay in state that afternoon and night in the big front room of the Hook Nine ranchhouse. Word of the killing had spread far and wide. Ranchers came from as far away as the Tenkiller Crossing of the Illinois River, and from the region near the mouth of the Sans Bois on the Choctaw nation side. Indian Joe and his wife came.

Full-blooded Cherokees and Choctaws mingled, then formed a line and entered the ranchhouse to pay their respects. Sue Bowman had expressed a desire to

111

stay and help out, and Boot drove the little gray horse and the buggy to the barnlot, unhitched the horse and fed and watered it. Sue helped Lawana prepare a meal for the visitors. Another night went by and no one slept.

Early next morning, Sue Bowman left the ranch, but when the funeral procession had wound down from the uplands, across the bottoms to the Sixkiller cemetery, she was there, wearing a small black hat with a single ostrich plume and appropriate black dress with white lace trim.

The caskets stood beside the open graves in the shade of the tall trees. Men and women formed a choir and sang. Boot stood with his mind caught up in sad retrospect while the voice of the preacher droned on and on.

A hand touched his arm, and he looked down into the face of Sue Bowman. "I feel that someone ought to walk with you, Mr. Lantry, if you don't mind."

The extent of his deep introspection suddenly struck him then. "Where's Lawana?" he said.

"She fainted, Mr. Lantry, but the women are taking care of her." Sue Bowman paused a moment. "The caskets are open now."

A long line of people was forming, filing past the caskets for a last look at the dead. Boot walked out and joined the end of the line, Sue Bowman beside him.

He paused at each casket and had his look, and lifted his gaze to see the northern foothills through a shimmering misty veil. He turned and looked once again into the still faces of his brother and father, and remembered that they had been murdered, and again his desire for vengeance almost overrode his grief.

He moved away, not conscious that Sue Bowman was slowly following him. The knuckles of his hand showed white against the tightly held curled brim of his hat. He finally put on the hat and pulled it down square and tight, and stood looking eastward, toward the tops of brick and frame buildings that marked Fort Smith.

A stir of dust on the Fort Smith—Tahlequah road suddenly caught his attention. He saw a shiny new hack approaching, pulled by a team of sleekly matched bays. The team was coming at a fast clip, turning abruptly into the cemetery drive.

The harnesses of the team looked polished. The huge brass nubs of the hames glittered in the morning sun. Boot drew himself up straight, his glance riveted on the two persons riding in the front seat of the hack. He instantly recognized Ina Jansen. Wes Cutler was driving the team.

The outrage of their late arrival would have made Boot resentful, even had they not been together. The hack halted at the edge of the crowd, but not before Boot had wheeled around.

He saw Sloan Vestal and the preacher, standing quietly beside the open caskets, waiting while a half dozen tottery elders shambled past.

"The funeral's over!" Boot called sharply. "Close up the coffins now!"

The preacher stared at Boot, and so did Sloan Vestal. Sloan finally said, "Why, boss, there are other visitors coming. Miss Jansen yonder, and Wes Cutler. I—"

"I said close them up!"

His voice carried across the crowd, crackling like a whiplash. He was conscious that all eyes were turned toward him, staring at him, but he took the impact of Sue Bowman's unbelieving look, and the chiding look of the preacher as well, and he was still a determined and angered man. He kept his own gaze fastened steadily upon Sloan Vestal, silently and significantly commanding the Hook Nine man to get to work.

Vestal nervously began to screw down the lids of the coffins. Boot motioned other Hook Nine hands forward, gesturing for them to lower the caskets into the graves.

"I just can't believe it of you, Mr. Lantry!" Sue Bowman whispered. "This is such a cruel and unfeeling thing to do."

Boot left her without an answer or a backward look, and headed straight toward Ina and Wes Cutler.

He said to Cutler, "Turn that team around and get out of here! Didn't I warn you yesterday to keep off Lantry land?"

Cutler's gloved hands tightened on the checklines. He glanced sideward at Ina's tense face.

"We just came to pay our respects to neighbors, Lantry," Wes Cutler said.

"There's a lot wrapped up in the word neighbor," Boot Lantry said. "Pa and No Fire were never neighbors of yours. Neither was I!"

Ina Jansen gasped and lifted a shaking hand to her throat. "Boot, you're awful. You're saying an awful thing."

There was a deep soul-sickness in Boot Lantry, but he wouldn't even look at her. He said again to Cutler,

114

"Turn your team and get that rig out of here!"

He stood with boots firmly planted in the dirt of the Sixkiller family plot and watched Cutler turn the team and go.

He was still standing that way when Sue Bowman hurried past him, lifting the hem of her black skirt above the dusty grass and weeds. He watched her step up to the buggy seat and lift the checklines of the little iron-gray horse with the one albino eye. It was strange; there was a breathless hope in him that she would turn and look back at him, but she never did. She slapped the rump of the gray with the checklines and drove away fast on the road toward Fort Smith.

# Chapter Eleven

Folks were to tell for years how the Hook Nine men came riding, thundering across the valley with Boot Lantry in the lead.

Pistol butts rested firm in tied-down holsters. The polished walnut stocks of rifles glistened in the sun above the mouths of saddle boots. The men rode like a charge of cavalry, almost splashing the pool dry at the Garrison Creek crossing as they thundered through and surged on along the road up Old Payne's Mountain and down the side road that led to Wes Cutler's ranch.

Behind them rode a close-knit group of U. S. deputy marshals, but everyone knew the presence of the marshals was more to keep down gunplay than it was a killer quest.

Everyone knew it, or sensed it, except Indian Joe.

Indian Joe saw the riders and wondered about them, because his mind, his whole body it seemed, was bent upon wondering about things on this pleasant sunny afternoon.

It was strange the way whiskey hit a man's stomach and sent its power tingling along the muscles, then backed up like a crawfish and made a sudden rerun and put dreaming and vast expectations into the brain. And it made a man happy and wondering, or maybe sad and a little fearful all in the same instant, because in spite of all the wonder, and the enhanced beauty of things, whiskey was wrong and it made men pig-shoat crazy afterwards.

Indian Joe had seen men afterwards, sick as grass-eating dogs.

He lifted a bottle to his lips and took a swig of the smuggled hooch.

"I be sick-hell tomor'," he said to no one. He took another nip and then stooped beside the sumac thicket, laid the bottle flat on the ground and covered it with leaves. He broke the tops from two bushes, tossing the hard clusters of berries from him, to mark a place he was fully aware he might soon forget.

He went at a shambling walk down the side of Old Payne's Mountain, and reached his spotted horse in the shade of the elm tree.

"I go watch that Lantry man," he said as he untied the horse, threw reins over its neck and pulled himself to the time-darkened leather seat of the saddle. Indian Joe sat a moment, his head tilted back, grinning up at the cobalt blue of the sky. "That Lantry, him big fine man, look like. Got good hoss, too."

Indian Joe let all the riders clatter past on the road below him, then put the spotted horse to a gallop, following in their wake. He was fairly close behind the entire group when they pulled up in front of Cutler's house.

Wes Cutler was coming out the doorway by the time Indian Joe rode up and joined the Hook Nine riders and the marshals. But Joe didn't pay much mind to Cutler. He kept looking warily at the deputy marshals, and some of them in turn looked suspiciously back at him.

"I not drunk," Indian Joe said. He belched "Got stomach growl. Drink pokeberry juice. No drink much whis'. Not much."

"You be quiet, Joe," one of the marshals said.

Wes Cutler said from the high veranda, "Good afternoon, gentlemen. Get down and come in."

Indian Joe forgot himself instantly then, because he was looking at Boot Lantry. Indian Joe had seen the urge to kill in the eyes and faces of many men, and he saw the urge now in the flare of Lantry's eyes and the cast of his young but rugged features. Or was the whiskey causing Indian Joe to perceive things that were not really there?

Indian Joe wondered. Boot Lantry's voice was quiet enough.

"This isn't a friendly visit, Cutler. I want to ask you some questions that I didn't ask this morning when you rode your hack to the funeral. Step out here, close to the yard fence, so I can see you close."

Cutler swallowed. He looked at Boot, then at the group of Hook Nine riders, at the deputy marshals, and finally back to Boot. Cutler raised a hand and braced it against one of the square posts of the porch.

"I don't have to answer questions from you,

Lantry. After that insult this morning—right in front of the woman I'm going to marry—I'm reluctant to even show the courtesy of talking to you at all."

Indian Joe wished that white men wouldn't use words he couldn't understand. He belched.

One of the deputy marshals spurred his mount close to the yard gate. "Answer Lantry's questions, Cutler."

Cutler winced. He looked out over the corrals and beyond them. He scanned the mountain slopes. He had been caught alone, and it was plain that he didn't like it. It was plain, even to Indian Joe.

But Indian Joe was getting steadily drunker. The whole scene was becoming a little befogged.

"Wes Cutler buy lease to lan'," Indian Joe said thickly. "Him give good saddle, hoss, lotsa dolla." Indian Joe patted the neck of his spotted horse. He glanced at the deputy marshals. "I no drink much whis'. Not much."

"Shut up!" one of the deputy marshals said.

Cutler was leaning forward, almost over the porch edge. "What . . . what is it you want to know, Lantry?"

"You know what I want to know!"

"I don't. I'll swear I don't."

"I want you to tell me exactly where you were about sundown, two days ago—and I want you to furnish proof."

"You don't suspect?"

"Yes, I do!"

Cutler licked his blue-tinged lips. Suddenly they looked dry, weathered, wind-cracked. "I couldn't

120

furnish satisfactory proof. Not anyone you would believe. My riders, you wouldn't?"

"Hell, no!"

Indian Joe leaned back on his horse and laughed. He wasn't aware that it had a sound like that of a whinnying mule. Indian Joe was deliriously drunk. He slapped his thigh.

"Cutler, him hav' good time two nights ago," Indian Joe said. "Cutler ride hack up hill, take woman with him, all way top Ol' Payne."

Boot Lantry's impatient voice lashed at the Indian, "When? What time?"

Indian Joe's face turned serious. His eyes moved sideward, throwing his dark, introspective and drunken glance under the belly of Lantry's horse.

"Cutler go on hack ride with Jansen girl. She pretty girl, too, look like! I pick pokeberries on hill, watch Cutler—"

Lantry's voice pounded at him. "What time, Joe?"

"Well, we on Payne hill. 'Bout sundown. Dark maybe. Maybe moon up. I see plain."

"Are you sure that wasn't last night?" Boot demanded.

Indian Joe shook his head. "Not las' night. Las' night I go Fort Town, buy hooch!"

Boot reined Taw up close to the Indian, watching Indian Joe's face with a rapier gaze. "Joe, this is one time you have to be certain you're right. You have to be sure you're right about the time, about the place. You understand? You have to be certain, Joe. You think on that."

"Sundown," Joe said firmly. "No moonshine yet. Cutler, him stand on hill, squeeze girl good,

121

ummmm, hug big! I laugh, shakum bush, make scare, hav' me some fun. I go down house, say, 'Ol' woman, I hug you big, you cook me grub!' I not drink much whis'. Not much!''

It was a little amazing to Indian Joe, but Lantry was turning his big horse away and the whole scene was disintegrating, with all the deputy marshals and the Hook Nine riders leaving their places beside the yard fence.

Indian Joe blinked rapidly, and swiped a hand down from his forehead and across his eyes. He turned in his saddle, almost toppling to the ground in the process, and watched the long string of riders galloping back toward the valley road that led to Whiskey Smith.

"I need drink whis'," Joe muttered.

Then dimly he saw Wes Cutler, standing there at the yard gate, just a few feet away.

"I was wondering how I'd ever get even with you on that deal we made about Garrison Creek land," Cutler said. There was hardness in his eyes and on his face, and Indian Joe was befogged and puzzled. "But I'll call it even now. You saved my life, no doubt. Because if I was on Payne's Mountain at sundown, I couldn't have been near the Lantry Ranch—get the hell out of here!''

Indian Joe slowly turned his horse, feeling impelled to try to overtake Lantry and the other riders, but knowing full well he was no longer capable of riding a fast-traveling horse. Indian Joe felt defeated. He wanted to cry.

But he still had enough sense left to find the sumac thicket. He slid off the spotted horse and began crawling, patting the leafy earth.

He crawled, and crawled some more and patted and patted. He looked bewildered, then frustrated, then angry. He glanced around, and saw the flat, bare feet and fat legs of his wife nearby.

She leaned down at him, shaking the half-filled bottle of whiskey in his face.

"You want some drink this whis', Joe?"

Joe's face brightened. He shut one eye, and the other nodded.

His fat wife leaned closer. "You want big drink this here good whis' now, Joe?"

"I need good drink, ol' woman. Need lots that whis'!"

She giggled and gave it to him, the whole contents of the bottle, sloshing against his nose, down past his mouth, drenching his dirty clothes.


Lantry and the Hook Nine riders, still accompanied by the deputy marshals, halted in the yard at the Jansen home. Boot dismounted and went up the rough stone steps and onto the porch.

Ina Jansen came through the doorway and met him. She twisted her hands in her apron, looked at Boot, then past him. "What does all this mean?"

"Nothing to get excited about, Ina. Where's Sully?"

"Why, I haven't seen my brother all week long. Not since the day you first rode home."

"Do you have any idea where we might find him?"

"No. I don't have any idea at all. What do you want with him?"

123

"Maybe nothing. Maybe a lot," Boot said. "If he does come home, tell him he better come and see me, pretty quick."

"Why?" Ina looked at the deputy marshals. "What has Sully done?"

Boot turned from her. "I just need to talk to him. You tell him so."

He was mounting again when he saw old Tobe Jansen, tramping through the weeds from the direction of the creek. Boot reined that way and stopped.

"Have you seen Sully recently?"

Old Tobe stood still in his patched clothes. "I don't know anything about that unruly kid, and don't want to know anything. He's a flat, low-down no-good!"

"You're not very partial to that son of yours, are you, Tobe?"

Old Tobe merely glared. Then, when Lantry was turning his horse, Tobe Jansen called out, loud and clear: "Say, ain't tomorrow the hanging day? Old Jeb's hanging, I mean?"

Boot's stomach crawled. He barely nodded, then a thought came to him, and he said, "You ought to find Sully and bring him in to witness it. Sight of a hanging might do Sully good."

He joined the Hook Nine men and the deputy marshals. They splashed back across the creek. Boot led the cavalcade, riding slower because the urgency in this direction was no more. A deputy marshal said beside him, "Tomorrow when the crowds gather is the time to be on watch. Sometimes the look in a man's eyes tells the tale."

Boot dipped his head. "Yep. Unless the killers are hardened, or naturally born that way."

He was thinking of Mace Bracken and Hemp Surate as he spoke.

The deputy marshals parted company with Hook Nine at the old ranch road, and traveled on leisurely toward Fort Smith. Boot led the Hook Nine riders a short distance and halted. He said to Sloan Vestal, "Take the men and head back to the ranch. I'll see you later tonight."

Vestal's tense face lifted. "Boot, we'll side you, wherever you travel."

"I know that, Sloan. But tonight there's no need. You fellows go get some rest."

"What about yourself?"

"I couldn't sleep." Boot left them, turning back in the direction of Fort Smith.

He rode slower, not wanting to take the chance of overtaking the deputy marshals. When he reached the forks near the river, he turned right on the road that led through Moffett.

He would cross by way of the Choctaw Wharf, he thought. His gray eyes glinted. In his mind he was seeing the crowded, smoke-filled barroom of Hemp Surate's place on Smoky Row.

It was nearing sundown. He rode down the steep embankment to the gravel bar that made the ferry landing on the Cherokee nation side. Luckily, the ferry was stopped there, waiting for a couple of ramshackle wagons to be pulled off by stubborn ox teams. Across the river, Boot saw the bright sheen of water at the Poteau's mouth, and the huddle of shanties of Cocaine Hill, like a dirt-dauber's nest on

125

the Point.

Twilight was creeping along the river, and a dank, chilly fog was rising from the water by the time the ferry crossed and touched at the flat rock of Choctaw Wharf. Boot paid his fare to the thick-chested Indian, led Taw off and mounted. Above the rush of the joining rivers, he heard a child crying somewhere up on Cocaine Hill.

Boot wouldn't look at the old Jansen shanty. The aggravating hurt and sickness was still in him. He passed the shanty and stopped Taw at the rail in front of Hemp Surate's place.

Among the thick cluttering of saddled horses and bareback ponies he was reluctant to leave Taw free. He looped the reins over the tie-rail and jerked a knot in them, and let his hand slide affectionately along the big black's neck before he entered the blind tiger saloon's narrow door.

A washing of commingling sound pushed against him, but somehow muted, as if all the gossip in the Indian nations lay packed inside the room and had stifled itself with its own foul volume. Then he saw Hemp Surate behind the bar, turned slightly in the other direction, and he heard Hemp's voice:

"You're a rotten braggart, Sully. You look like killing someone!"

"I'll kill him, if it's the last thing I ever do! I don't go for this stuff of havin' my gun snatched off me! I'll kill him! Wouldn't you kill him, Mace, if you was me?"

Boot couldn't see Mace Bracken through the thick and shifting crowd, but he heard him curse, and then heard his harsh rejoinder, "I expect I would, Sully. It

126

ain't a very pleasant thing to have your gun taken away."

"Sully's still a snotnose braggart," Hemp Surate snarled. "Besides all that, he's drunk!"

Boot caught a glimpse of Sully's face. The kid was sitting on a bar stool, his elbows propped on the rough oak bar. And Mace Bracken was just beyond him, standing with a whiskey glass in one hand.

Boot Lantry stood just inside the doorway, letting their heated exchange of words slither off the surface of his thoughts. He looked the dingy room over, thinking of the Dakin boys and his mind shot through with memories of a time two years ago.

Signs of the crashing brawl and gun fight had been erased by a cheap coating of paint, another plank in the floor and another second-hand back-bar mirror. But scars on the minds of the Dakin boys might never be erased so easily. Old Jim Bill Dakin's sons would remember this room as a trap for a frame-up, and maybe as a trap for murder. And Hemp Surate, with his knife-scarred, brutish face—what would he remember it for?

Boot's presence at the door had suddenly been sensed. The noise in the room diminished. Someone cleared his throat and coughed. Hemp Surate turned about, his head jerking up like that of a puppet heaved by a hidden string.

He moved rapidly from behind the bar and approached Boot. His black eyes under heavy brows were slightly protuberant, and they had a shining brilliance even in the dimness.

"I won't have trouble here, Lantry! You know what happened once. What are you doing here?"

Lantry merely stared coldly at him, noticing the restless, sideward cast of Surate's eyes. Hemp wouldn't meet Lantry's gaze head-on. It was a mannerism odd for Hemp Surate. A man could mistake it for fear, Lantry thought.

The crowd was silent, and Sully was sitting still on the stool at the bar. Mace Bracken was the only one moving. He came up behind Hemp Surate and stopped. Bracken's face was pale and filled with a subtle rashness that was intensified by the shine of his whiskey-brightened eyes.

Mace had a pistol on him, Boot noticed. The gun was thrust inside his belt on the left side, butt forward for a right-hand pull.

Boot's glance drilled him, and then flashed past him to Sully Jansen.

"Step outside, Sully. I want to talk to you."

If Sully had been drunk, he obviously had sobered swiftly. He stood up. When he did, one of his elbows knocked a whiskey glass over. The glass rolled along the bar edge, then crashed to smithereens against the floor.

Sully had been on the verge of jerking his pistol. Boot had sensed it the instant Sully stood up. But the crash of the glass unnerved him. He stood with his hand poised above the butt of his pistol, blinking his eyes rapidly and licking his lips.

Boot's voice, wedge-hard and sharp, slammed against him. "You better remember what I told you, Sully. About kids that fill early graves. If you touch that gun I'll have to kill you! Now step on out, where I can talk to you."

Boot had made up his mind that any hesitation on

his part could bring death here, either to himself or others. His right hand dropped and came darting up, freighted with his Colt. He let the muzzle of the gun slant as much toward Mace Bracken as toward Sully, because he had sensed that Mace Bracken had murder in his whiskey-sodden brain.

Sight of the big Colt in Lantry's hand had a certain power of persuasion, evidently. Sully Jansen's hands fell limply and he started walking with downcast eyes toward the door.

"Turn around, Mace!" Lantry ordered. "Turn around and face that bar."

Mace Bracken slowly and suddenly obeyed.

"Go side him, Surate. Turn your back to me."

Hemp Surate's protuberant eyes had a seething, malignant rage in them as he turned about and moved close to Mace. They were standing that way, bellied up against the bar stiff as ramrods, as Boot Lantry backed outside. There he faced around.

"Keep moving, Sully." Boot gestured. "On down toward the rock."

Sully kept walking. Boot followed, taking time to unwrap Taw's reins when he reached the tie-rail. Boot kept his gun in his hand, leading the horse behind Sully as Sully walked on down the twisting trail toward the Choctaw Wharf.

"That's far enough, Sully." Boot holstered his pistol. "Now you answer some questions. Where did you ride to, late that afternoon, after I met you on Garrison Creek?"

"I rode on home."

"You're lying! Your pa or Ina didn't see you there!"

129

Sully swallowed rapidly and kept blinking his eyes in the half darkness. "I . . . I slipped home an' slept in th' barn."

"Can you prove it? Did anyone see you?"

"I don't guess so," Sully said.

"You're lying, Sully. And it's going to get you in the worst bind you've ever been in. You know who killed my pa and No Fire, don't you?"

Sully's face got that weasel's look, sharp and drawn and taunting. "You can't wring nothing out of me. I know you ain't gonna shoot me. I know you won't do it, because I ain't gonna draw on you!"

The fury in Boot Lantry broke its leashes. He leaped at Sully and collared him, flinging him to the ground. He stooped, jerking Sully's pistol free of the scabbard and pushing it firmly down between his own belt and shirt. He caught Sully's dingy collar and hauled him up, and put a knee into his spine.

Boot left Taw standing at the river's edge with trailing reins and forced Sully at a rapid march up a cluttered alley of the Coke Hill district and on across the dip past the commissary building and thus to the federal courthouse. He kneed Sully up the high steps toward the U. S. marshal's quarters and shoved him roughly inside.

The wiry, keen-eyed and nervy deputy marshal with whom Boot had exchanged sharp words on the courthouse steps was on duty. His glance rested against Sully, then lifted to hold upon Boot's face. Reaves' eyes held a touch of mockery.

"So," the deputy marshal murmured. "Now it's you that's bringing in the kids."

Boot laid it on the line, neatly and swiftly, without

130

any embarrassment. "It could be I've been a foolish man. I may have some apologies to make to other deputy marshals, and even to Judge Parker, for the criticism I voiced about the stand he is making here."

"What has the kid here done?" Reaves asked.

"I'm not certain. Nothing too bad, yet, I hope. But I want you to hold him here until tomorrow. I want him to see that hanging done."

"Fentress?"

"Yes." Boot took Sully's pistol from his belt and handed it to the deputy marshal.

"You want me to throw the kid in jail?"

"No. No, not that. Just keep him awake in here tonight, right beside you. Let him listen to the prisoners moaning down in that dungeon. That sound, and the sight of old Jeb hanging, may do Sully a lot of good."

# Chapter Twelve

Garrison Street was dusty and cut by wheels of wagons and the hoofs of mules and horses. Stirred dust lay heavy between the saloons and other business houses, or swirled away in blinding palls through the alleys as puffs of autumn wind whipped in from across the Arkansas.

Boot Lantry and the Hook Nine riders traveled at a slow walk up the slope of the street from the commercial crossing. Sloan Vestal was riding by Boot's side. No one carried guns.

They passed the commissary building and the Le Flore Hotel, and the cluster of livery corrals on the left. The old opera house at the corner of Fifth and Garrison was plastered with pictures of wild west showmen, all commingled with very faded and aging placards advertising the appearance of the Swedish Nightingale, Jenny Lind.

Young Cherokee and Choctaw Indians stood

stoical-faced and silent under the multicolored marquee, but they weren't interested in what would take place on stage at the show. They watched the fronts of the saloons and wiped hands across their thirsty lips, and waited, hoping, hoping, hoping. But no one would buy them drinks. No one. If Indians wanted drinks they had to go to places like Hemp Surate's blind tiger, where knives too often flashed, and six-shooters roared, and dead bodies weighted with sacks of rocks or sand could be hurriedly dumped into the Poteau river or the Arkansas. That was the way it was.

Crowds of people surged in and out of the stores and others paced the sidewalks. There were sagging planks across the dust of Garrison Street and the planks were crowded too, as people crossed to and fro.

"Well, it looks like it takes a hanging to bring folks—to stir them out."

Sloan Vestal's voice was tense and low.

Boot merely nodded. He had recognized two faces in the stream of people crossing the avenue. His gaze followed them.

Evidently they had just stepped from the front of Napier's Funeral Parlor. Sue Bowman was carrying two large wreaths of flowers, and Mace Bracken was carrying two more.

They crossed to Sue Bowman's buggy on the street's southern edge. Mace Bracken was wearing a new dark beaver hat, a blue-serge frock coat, and a stiff-collared shirt with a black string tie. His trousers were neatly pressed and his feet appeared deceptively small and elegant in new patent-leather shoes. What a contrast from the night before, Boot thought.

134

Then he noticed the slight bulge under Mace's coat on the left side, and he knew Mace's pistol was there.

The two were talking, seemingly oblivious to the passing crowds or the approach of the Hook Nine riders, as they placed the wreaths in the buggy, then moved up to the shade of an awning that thrust out from the front of a hardware store.

"Take the men and wait over on the north side," Boot told Vestal, and didn't wait for a reply. He reined to the south, directly in front of Sue and Mace, and halted Taw.

"I thought I ought to tell you, Mace. Bring out the family hack."

Bracken squared his shoulders. The accustomed hate and rashness filled his eyes. It intensified when he saw Boot wasn't armed.

"This is one show you don't run, Lantry. Fentress made all arrangements himself. All of them!"

Lantry's boots pushed hard into the stirrups. In the temporary quietness the saddle creaked. "As far as I'm concerned, Jeb Fentress is still a part of Hook Nine. I'll be setting the policies and paying for the extras at his funeral, hours after Jeb is dead. He's never said it, but he's been so much a part of Hook Nine, I know he'd expect it. So bring out the family hack."

Bracken stepped forward in fury. "I won't do any such goddamn thing!"

Lantry was watching Bracken steadily, but he was conscious that Sue Bowman had caught her breath and wheeled around.

"Why, Mr. Bracken! Of course you'll bring out the hack. It would be callous of the funeral home not to, don't you think?"

"I don't give a thin damn what's callous or what ain't callous!" Bracken flared.

"Why, Mr. Bracken, I'm amazed!" Her blue eyes flashed up at Lantry. "Lawana will come, won't she? She'll want to ride the hack?"

"That's the reason I'm ordering it, Miss Bowman. For Lawana and myself."

Bracken's right hand streaked up to grab the brim of his beaver, then released and dropped and caught a clamping hold on the lapel of his coat. Lantry's cold gaze held him, like a fly in a spider's trap.

"Have the hack at the courthouse, in the funeral procession, Mace. And have it in its proper place." Lantry started to turn Taw, then stopped. "And you don't go with the hack, Mace. Old Jim Bill Dakin will do the driving. You don't step onto our land, Mace. Remember? Remember what I said?"

Mace's curse was sibilant, like the hiss of a snake, as Boot rode away.

Horsebackers, wagons and buggies, and a swank phaeton or two were pouring off the junction of the Texas Road and roiling up the dust of Garrison Street. People were coming from the Choctaw nation by the hundreds, down from the Ozarks out of the bottomlands of western Arkansas.

They were crowding the ferries from the Cherokee nation, lean and quick eyed men from Webbers Falls, Gore and Tahlequah, and the hell-raising town of Vian at the foot of the Cookson Hills.

Lantry rejoined his riders and motioned back westward.

"It's about time. Let's go."

They rode back to where the street pitched down toward the river. There they turned and rode to the next street southward. They halted near the old brick barracks building that housed the Federal courtroom and the infamous dungeon jail.

Boot dismounted, and the sight that met his vision made him stand a moment, rigid, outraged and appalled. This was a garish picnic, a carnival, complete with hawkers, lemonade and all.

Any permits to witness the hanging would have been a farce, he knew.

Swarms of people crowded the jail-yard walls and dozens sat perched atop the walls like vultures, their heads and necks moving, straining, and their lips opening and closing on talk as they looked at the sloping roof of the gibbet and the vast beam that could accommodate a dozen ropes and twelve condemned men at one drop. Others drank soda pop, or laughed and conversed in the shade.

"Wait here, Sloan. I'll bring Sully out. And I want every Hook Nine man to keep an eye on him. Watch his reactions. Watch him like hawks."

The marshal's quarters were crowded. Sully was sitting nervously in a corner, chewing his fingernails. Boot spoke to a marshal briefly, and the marshal looked at Sully and nodded.

"I'll walk to the gallows with old Jeb, Sully. You can watch it all with the Hook Nine crew. Let's go," Boot said.

Sully got up. "You sound damned biggety, ordering me around this way. When can I get my gun?"

"After it's over, maybe. Then maybe you can come

get your gun and be on your way."

Boot led the way to where the Hook Nine men waited and left Sully there, and turned back toward the entrance of the basement dungeon jail.

But a cackling laugh made him turn again, and when he turned he saw Tobe Jansen. Old Tobe had just stepped out from the crowd and joined Sully.

"This ain't just hangin' day, it's faintin' day!" Tobe Jansen said. There was a shrill resonance in his voice that sliced through the noise of the crowd. He was looking straight at Boot, tauntingly and jeeringly. "You're fixing to side a man that will never be game enough to walk them thirteen steps. Everyone always talked about good ol' stout-hearted Jeb Fentress, but you'll find out soon that talk didn't mean a thing!"

Lantry's long stride took him across the grass to confront Jansen. Boot said savagely, "What are you trying to stir up here, you old goat?"

The Adam's apple danced up and down in Jansen's throat. He cackled a laugh again.

"You ain't deaf. You hear me. I'll bet good money that Jeb Fentress faints before they get the rope around his neck!"

Boot's full lips twisted slightly. "I'd hate to think of what you would do, old man, if you had to face the thing Jeb Fentress is facing. We couldn't stand the smell of your pants!"

Jansen's face paled. "You git away from me, Lantry! I'm damned glad I ain't gonna have you for a son-in-law."

Boot's gaze held upon him, but he wasn't really seeing Tobe Jansen. Boot was seeing two women,

138

comparing them, and the thing that raced across his vision was revelation, bright and warm and comforting even in this moment of stress.

"I'm glad too, Jansen," Boot Lantry said. "I sure am."

He faced the jail entrance again and saw old Jeb. They were bringing him out, handcuffed to the burly deputy marshal Boot had met that first day. Other deputy marshals and a priest were gathered, standing in groups beside the high iron door.

Boot stepped quickly forward, conscious that the alert eyes of the deputy marshals were upon him. He reached old Jeb and offered his hand. The old man responded with his left one. His right hand wasn't free.

Boot didn't say anything. Neither did Fentress. Boot released the hand and squared around beside Jeb. He walked with him as far as the gibbet. There he felt his arms caught by a deputy marshal. Boot stopped and watched the firm stride of Jeb's boots, and heard the strokes of the bootheels on the steps, lifting up faint echoes, like the wooden chimes of doom.

There was only one rope dangling from the gibbet beam after all. That was good, Boot thought. The raging prisoner inside the jail had not known what he was talking about. Old Jeb could die with a certain dignity. Whining, crying, terrified common criminals up there beside him would have changed the picture. It was possible they would have made it harder for old Jeb.

Boot glanced around and saw the crowd had thickened. Sloan Vestal and the Hook Nine men had done their job. They had pushed Sully Jansen right up to the front where the kid was bound to see it all.

Jeb Fentress was on the platform. The priest and the marshals stood by his side. The robe of the priest whipped in the sharp October wind as Jeb looked over the crowd.

He seemed to be a calm man, surprisingly calm for a man facing the door of death. He looked at Boot and at Sloan Vestal, then at all his former riding companions, the men he had bossed on the ranch. He looked at their faces one by one, and his own face had a look of compassion for them, as if the impact of this terrible incident would hurt them worse than it would hurt him.

His expression didn't alter until he looked at Sully Jansen. Then suddenly there was more than compassion in his face. It was something instant and unreadable, instantly noticed by Boot but not wholly recognized. It was a puzzling expression, half hope, half agony. It all appeared fleetingly on old Jeb's face, then was as swiftly erased.

"Would you like to say something, Mr. Fentress?" one of the marshals asked.

Old Jeb was a sensitive man, and prideful—a man of deep insight. "Last words are pretty futile, marshal, but I would like to say one thing. People ought to make the best of their lives here on earth. We're a short time here and a long time gone."

He was still looking down at young Sully. Boot looked sideward at Sully and saw that the kid's face was as hard as flint and almost as white as the rocks that dotted the Cherokee Hills.

Things moved swiftly after that. The deputy

140

marshals were binding Jeb's legs and hands and adjusting the rope about his neck when a Choctaw Indian said in a guttural voice, "Whar Maledon? Whar that hangman at?"

His question was directed to no one in particular, but it was an urgent one. The Choctaw's glance swept away from the men adjusting the loop and flashed at the man who was standing to the left of the gibbet, waiting to jerk the trapdoor pins.

George Maledon was not here. The old Bavarian hangman who had sent so many men to their instant doom, almost without a twitch, was not on hand. Another hangman was taking his place.

Maledon's absence was enough to cause concern in Boot Lantry. His glance quested through the crowd. He picked out a U. S. marshal and swiftly moved close to him.

"Why isn't Maledon here?"

"He refused to hang Fentress," the marshal answered. "He told the judge he didn't think Fentress was guilty. Besides, Maledon said he wouldn't hang Fentress because they fought in the War together, in the same regiment."

When Boot looked back toward the gibbet, he saw that the marshals were adjusting Jeb's mask.

He was a faceless figure, tall and straight in heavy boots, his hands tied and his feet bound, standing on the trapdoor with the rope around his neck. Whispering had been racing through the crowd, but now it stopped, and the metallic rasp of the trapdoor pin was like the sound of a powder blast in that waiting silence.

Jeb dropped to the end of the rope and writhed

141

there, slowly strangling to death.

There were things a man couldn't stand to see, and this was one of them. Boot had taken three strides toward the gibbet, opening his jackknife to cut the rope, when two marshals collared him.

It was the slam of a pistol barrel that downed Boot. He was down on the earth, on all fours, dizzy, half blinded but straining to gain his feet. He heard someone yelling, and there was something familiar about the sound, but at first he couldn't place it. Then, as his head cleared, he looked up and saw that it was Sully Jansen.

Sully was leaning forward, straining and shaking while two deputy marshals held his arms. Sully's convulsed face was set in the direction of old Jeb Fentress. Sully kept screaming, over and over, "Stop it! Someone stop it! My God, someone stop this thing!"

But no one stopped it. The crowd was vanishing, some of the people almost running across the grass around the gibbet stand. When Boot finally rose, his head clearing, he saw that Jeb was dead. Two doctors were standing beside him, pressing stethoscopes to his chest, listening at nothing. Jeb Fentress was no more.

# Chapter Thirteen

Sully Jansen staggered like someone half blinded into the U. S. marshal's quarters at the Federal courthouse. He skidded to a stop in his run-over boots and pushed his hands out pleadingly toward the jailer and two marshals.

"Please, I want my gun!" Sully choked.

They looked him over, gauging his excitement. "You look like a wild bronc has just throwed you sky-western-crooked," one of the marshals said.

Sully's young mouth quivered. "Can't I have my gun? Lantry said I could get it back and ride out of town as soon as the . . . that hangin' was over."

"All right, but I'm taking the loads out, and you'd be a wise kid to keep them in your pocket until you get back across the line. In fact, you'd be a wiser kid if you'd just get rid of the gun, cartridges and all, for good."

Sully started to say something, but choked on the

words. He jerked his head up and down. One of the marshals took the gun from a shelf, ejected the cartridges and handed belt, holster, gun and ammunition to Sully. The kid rammed the loads into his right rear pocket, slung the pistol, belt and holster over his shoulder, and left the courthouse almost at a run.

He didn't go past the gibbet, where deputy marshals and funeral directors were placing the body of Jeb Fentress in a coffin. Sully ducked his head and hurried away along the north end of the barracks building, passing the hearse and the family hack and the other vehicles in the procession.

He glanced up just once, and wanted to shut the faces of those in the procession out of his mind. There were too many families he recognized, too many men he had known and watched pass along to and from town and the ferry landings since he was small.

He saw old Jim Bill Dakin, sitting on the driver's side of the family hack, and Sully remembered the time old Jim Bill had tried to wrangle the truth out of him about Lute and Stafford. The sight of old Jim Bill's piercing eyes made Sully strike out into a run.

He raced through a crooked alley of Cocaine Hill. It appeared that the dirty squatters' domain was deserted, except for a few ragged kids here and there. Sully hurried on, ducking under the branches of a thick growth of willows. He reached the rocky shoreline of the river and finally stopped.

He flung his gun, scabbard and belt as far into the water as he could, then dug frantically in his hip pocket for the cartridges. He got them all in his right hand and hurled them, and watched the puny sprinkling they made on the surface of the stream.

Sully leaned over, gagged, and emitted a portion of his sickness on the rocks. At last, pale and weakened, he crossed the rocks of the old Choctaw Wharf, climbed the embankment on tottery legs, and went on to Hemp Surate's place on Smoky Row.

His searching glance found his gaunted pony, still standing at the tie-rail where it had stood all night long and almost half the day. Sight of the poor animal made Sully sick again, and he thought, Hemp or Mace wouldn't take time to feed him. Not ever. Not even if my pony stood here a week and died from hunger and thirst.

Sully moved quietly, untying the reins of the pony. He managed to mount, but his boots were dangling limply, and he was so exhausted and sick his hands were shaking and he could barely get hold of the reins again to guide the horse.

"Where you headin', kid?"

It was the voice of Hemp Surate. He was standing in the narrow doorway of his plank-and-batten blind tiger, his hard stare reaching at Sully, questing around Sully's waistline for Sully's gun.

"What did you do with your six-shooter, boy?"

Sully's lips were going dry. He licked them. Behind Hemp Surate he saw the leering face of Mace Bracken, and Sully knew they had not attended the hanging. They had stayed here in this dingy place drinking their whiskey while old Jeb Fentress died.

"I throwed my gun in the river," Sully said. "I'm through."

"Yeah?" Hemp Surate stepped out into the

sunlight, his shaggy, rust-colored hair catching the glare. "Through with what?"

"I'm through with everything," Sully said. "I'm goin' home. I ain't seen Ma in weeks."

Hemp stopped, watching Sully. "That hangin' must have shook you up." He laughed. "What if it had been your own necktie party, Sully? The whole works, rope and all, just for you?"

Sully was violently sick, and he was scared. Fear was a writhing serpent, deep in his guts. Fear was the sight of a man bouncing and jerking at the end of a rope—a man whose neck had not snapped, the victim of a bungled job of hanging, a man strangling to death.

"I'm goin' home," Sully repeated. "I'm ridin' home."

"Well, now, I reckon that's all right, Sully, just so you don't hang around your old lazy pa too long."

That was Mace Bracken speaking now. He had stepped out, too, and Sully saw that Mace cut a pretty good figure, dressed in his blue-serge suit and his white shirt and tie.

Sully started to ride again, but Mace had other things to say. "Hold on, now, kid. Tell your sister Ina that I may be coming out to try to court her again. I think Ina and me are going to kind of lose out on the plans we had, and maybe we're gonna need each other."

Sully's sick eyes got big. "Why, Ina will marry Cutler, I guess."

"I don't think she will," Mace drawled. "No, I sure don't think she will. You ride on home, and visit your folks a few days, and you remember something,

146

Sully. There's a big ol' monkey liable to jump on someone's back, and it ain't gonna be me—or Hemp!"

Sully Jansen was retching again as he rode on, passing the edge of Cocaine Hill. He was in a desperate hurry now to board the old Indian ferry, to get across past "Little Juarez" and the Sixkiller graveyard before the funeral procession crossed the river from the commercial section and lined out on the Fort Smith—Tahlequah road.

Sully thought, There'll be other riders, and maybe families in wagons, coming on the road across Garrison Creek. After I pass the graveyard, I'll take to the woods.

Sully would dodge the main road, on his way to see his ma. . . .

The coffin was loaded. Boot turned away from Sloan Vestal and the Hook Nine riders and saw the teams of the procession, tightening up behind the hearse. The family hack that he had requested of Mace Bracken was in place, with old Jim Bill Dakin driving. Boot squared his shoulders. He reached the hack, climbed into the rear seat and sank into cushioned shadows.

Old Jim Bill said in a strained voice, without turning, "I sure was sorry to see Jeb go that way. It was a hell of a way to die."

"Yes, a hell of a way, Jim Bill," Lantry said.

He thought of Taw, and looked toward the Hook Nine horses and saw Taw's lifted head. Taw's big eyes, round as the taw marbles that Boot had

147

thumbed in the doodgie games at school, were questing for his master. It was usually that way with Taw, especially around crowds of people, when Boot Lantry disappeared.

"Look yonder, Boot. Ain't that a pretty sight?" old Jim Bill said.

Boot faced ahead and saw Sue Bowman. She was dressed in black, and a lacy veil covered her dark hair and fell in small, neat ruffles down over her eyes. She was beside the hearse, her arms loaded with the four wreaths of flowers. The driver of the hearse, the same man who had driven the funeral wagon out to the Lantry ranch, was taking the flowers from her and placing them gently on top of Jeb Fentress's coffin. The driver closed the doors of the hearse then, and climbed back up to the seat.

Sue Bowman faced the family hack then, and Boot noticed her manner of urgency. He kept watching her. She stood a moment, apparently in indecision, then started walking. Boot was surprised that she was coming straight toward the hack in which he sat.

She stopped near the hack and leaned forward, looking in at him. "Hasn't Lawana arrived yet?"

Boot shook his head. "I left a wrangler to drive her to town. She said she would try to make it, but that she wasn't feeling quite up to another funeral. She said if she wasn't here on time she would be on her way to Tahlequah. Lawana will go back to live with her folks."

Sue Bowman lifted her veil. He could see the sorrow in her eyes, the hurt and the compassion.

"Mr. Lantry, it may seem presumptuous, but do you mind if I ride with you?"

Boot looked at her, feeling the breathtaking shock of her level gaze, and knowing again that crowding sense of amazement at the contradictory, unpredictable ways of women.

The veil was still lifted, and the bright sun clearly revealed her face. It was a rather large face, but delicately textured, and not too large for her tall, strong body, he thought. It wasn't the time or the place to be comparing one girl with another, but he was doing it, comparing her with Ina Jansen.

Boot opened the door of the hack and moved sideward.

"I'll be happy to have you ride with me, Miss Bowman. Come in."

He reached to take her slim, cool hand, and she came up and settled herself beside him.

"Thank you, Mr. Lantry," she said. She released her hand and closed the door, and sat facing the crowd.

Boot let his own glance drift that way and he saw Mace Bracken. Mace was striding across the courthouse lawn from the direction of Smoky Row. He had a whiskey glass in his hand, and as he passed the gibbet he emptied it and carelessly tossed the glass toward the gallows stairs. His lightly protruding teeth, white as those of a wolf after a bone-chewing orgy, flashed in the high-riding sun.

The procession was starting. Boot felt the pressure of the rear of the seat against his shoulders and spine. Mace Bracken had reached the edge of the street and had stopped to stare in at Boot and Sue Bowman. Mace's eyes were wide open, letting the jealousy and hatred spill out.

149

Boot glanced sideward at Sue Bowman's face in profile and saw that her long lashes had dropped, veiling her eyes. Her lips were pressed together and her face looked pale. Mace Bracken's presence had disturbed her, Boot thought.

His own grim face set ahead. He and Sue Bowman rode quietly with the procession, on down to the ferry wharf.

It took some time to shuttle the procession across. Boot's tension mounted. He was thinking of Pa and No Fire, buried just a short time before, and of old Jeb Fentress, whose body would soon be six feet under the turf of Indian Territory in the Sixkiller family plot.

Boot Lantry had traveled hard and fast for many weary miles, to help old Jeb and to visit with his family, but he had visited with his father and brother only briefly, and there had been no way to help old Jeb.

He looked unseeingly up the river, feeling a constriction in his throat and a burning in his eyes. A man could ride a long way on devious trails and clamp the sorrow down tight inside of him, but somehow, one way or another, it would all come out.

The crossing was finally made, and the miles of the dusty road ribboned out behind the procession. The cemetery was there and the procession was halting. Boot climbed out of the hack on his side and took off his hat, and went around to open the door for Sue Bowman. She came down lightly, resting a hand against his shoulder briefly. She stood beside him, looking at the halted hearse.

Boot looked at her again and thought how strange

it was that in this moment, somewhere deep in his mind, he should liken her to Ina Jansen. He had compared them and knew there was no resemblance between them, and he wondered about the sudden strange tangent of his thoughts. He guessed it was caused by the force of the thing that had filled his mind on the long, fast ride from the Verdigris: that Ina would be ready to side him, in any time of stress.

The scene ahead was a garish repeat, minus only one dead man. The coffin was out, resting across two velvet-draped wooden sawhorses. The same preacher was there, and the same choir.

The choir was singing the very same song.

The appearance of old Tobe and Ma Jansen was somehow a shocking thing, possibly because they were in such a hurry. They came from the road on foot and rushed along beside the vehicles of the funeral procession, old Tobe still stubble-bearded and wearing patched pants, Ma stooped and stumbling, wearing an ancient plumed hat and a frayed brown taffeta coat that was perhaps a quarter of a century old.

They pushed up close to the choir, old Tobe gripping Ma's arm. Boot watched them intently; he saw that Ma Jansen was trembling. She was getting old, aging much too fast, Boot thought. He was concerned, because he doubted that Ma Jansen could keep standing until the preacher was through.

But she did, and then the funeral directors were opening the casket. It wasn't until the lid was back and old Jeb's bearded face was visible that Ma Jansen screamed and fell at the edge of the grave.

Women from the crowd rushed to her with fans,

lifting her and carrying her to the shade. Sue Bowman left Boot's side to join them, and Boot saw her deftly helping to take off Ma's coat and make a pillow of it, unbuttoning the tight collar of Ma's dress so she could breathe more freely.

Old Tobe Jansen had turned and was leaning through the crowd of women to watch.

"Git up from thar, woman!" Jansen yelled in an insane way. "You bony old Jezebel! I know you birthed a whelp of a son by the man that's sprawled in that coffin! I've knowed it all these years, you hear?"

Deathly silence followed his outburst. Sue Bowman and the women who were bending over Ma, lifting her as she revived from the faint, turned to look at old Tobe.

Tobe Jansen charged among them and lifted Ma to her feet. Ma was trying to look at the coffin again, but old Tobe wouldn't let her. He led Ma swiftly from the cemetery, carrying her coat in one hand and holding her upright with the other. They vanished beyond an alder thicket and a rank growth of weeds, heading back toward the cabin above the bank of Garrison Creek.

A rumble of thunder sounded, northwest, beyond Old Payne's Mountain. Dark clouds rolled up, blotting out the brassy sky and the warm flame of the zenith sun. The vehicles on the return trip were scattered far behind the hack in which Boot Lantry and Sue Bowman rode. Old Jim Bill was driving fast.

Huge drops of rain were pounding the dust of the road before they reached the ferry. Sue Bowman turned, looking into Boot's face.

"Maybe the long dry spell is going to break," she said. "We sure need it—water for the range grass, and the streams. I looked over our horses early this morning. They're getting thin."

"You've been back out to the ranch?"

She smiled and lifted her veil, pinning it up and leaving it there. "I've moved back, Mr. Lantry. At first, after Dad was . . . gone, I didn't want to live in the Territory. But staying with kinfolks is no good. I'm going to live on the Circle S and carry on. You know, come to think of it, we'll be neighbors, won't we? The way it was between the Lantry family and the Bowman family, before Jeb Fentress . . ."

"Jeb Fentress didn't kill your dad." Boot wasn't looking at her as he said it. He was looking straight ahead. "I think I know who did."

# Chapter Fourteen

Silence was like a burdensome weight between them for several minutes. Then he felt Sue Bowman stir on the seat.

"Will you go to the ranch tonight, Mr. Lantry?"

"Maybe. But it's doubtful. It may be days."

"Why?"

"I have things to find out," Boot said. "I don't think I'll find them out sticking too close to the ranch."

"You must go home, Mr. Lantry," she said. "Your father and brother would want you there. You need to stay at the ranch, to take over, to—"

"There won't be any taking over." Boot faced her squarely. "Not anything that Sloan Vestal and the riders can't handle, rounding up the cattle and selling them."

"Selling?"

"Yes. The proceeds will be split with Lawana.

155

After that, I won't be here. My interests are up on the Verdigris."

"Oh," Sue said. That was all she said for a moment. Boot noticed that her hands were restless in her lap. Then she said in a low voice, "Ina Jansen hurt you, didn't she? Very deeply."

His glance flicked at her. "I'll get over it. And don't call me Mr. Lantry. He was my pa, and he's not around anymore. Call me Boot."

"All right. And you may call me Sue, if you want to. You're a hard and violent man, aren't you, Boot?"

He said evenly, "Ina raved about my violence. I don't want to hear the same thing from you."

They were facing each other. Boot saw the start of tears in Sue Bowman's eyes.

"But women have to take a stand against violence!" she said. "Women marry, and become mothers of children, and they don't want to live in constant fear that the men they love, the fathers of their children, may at any time be involved in gun fights that may leave them dead."

"I can understand that. But the *real* women side their men in spite of that fear. The *real* women, those of fortitude, always have. Besides, Ina is getting herself a pretty violent man in Mace Bracken's uncle, Wes Cutler. I think I have Cutler pegged. The only thing that may keep him from getting killed is that he's a coward. He dreads to face up to any man, if that man has a gun on his hip."

"But why shouldn't a man be afraid of guns? They're ugly things, deadly!"

Boot smiled with an almost sardonic twist of his lips. "A man that's afraid of guns shouldn't live in

156

Indian Territory. He ought to go back to the protected settlements, back East where life moves slow and safe." When Sue Bowman didn't say anything, he added, "That would be the kind of life you would want, I guess."

Sue shook her head. "No, I love this country. I think it's a fascinating place to live. But I do wish we had more law and order. And though I hate to know of what happened on the courtgrounds today, I believe Judge Parker is a dedicated man, doing a job that must be done. Don't you?"

Boot waited a moment. Racing through his mind was the picture his dying brother No Fire had left for Sloan Vestal to repeat—killers, crowding their horses out of the woods of ambush; three of them, and maybe more, because No Fire, dying, may not have seen all of them.

"Well, I rode back here with some pretty strong opinions against Judge Parker," Boot said. "But those opinions have been altered some. I agree. I expect he's doing a job that has to be done. But I've studied the records. I think too many Indians are being hanged in proportion to white men. I think the white intruders in the Indian nations are causing as much or more trouble than anyone else."

Sue forced a smile through her tears. "And intruders mean people like my father and myself. I should leave the Territory, shouldn't I?"

"I didn't say that."

"You feel it, though." She laughed, but it was devoid of humor. Then she said, "Perhaps I could use my wiles, though, and marry you for land rights. You know, white men come in and marry Indian girls, probably the way your grandfather did, so what would be wrong in a white girl coming in and marrying an Indian man?''

Boot smiled too. "You'd run into trouble, if you captured me. Our children would be hard pushed to claim land rights, because the degree of Indian blood would be getting pretty slim. My father was only an eighth.''

But they were looking at each other, and Boot saw the change in her expression, the darkening of her blue eyes, the waiting stillness on her face. He was conscious that the blood was rushing to his face, and he thought, These things strike like lightning . . . like a fast spring storm.

Abruptly, she reached across to grasp his hand.

"Mr. Lantry . . . Boot . . . if anything is to be done about the deaths of your father and brother, or about Jeb Fentress, leave it to the U. S. marshals, please! Don't do anything rash. I know your temper, know how you want to push things, but the law will take care of everything, if you'll just wait.''

He had barely been conscious of boarding the ferry, but now they were back in town and Jim Bill Dakin was halting the hack.

"Thanks for siding me, Sue," he said. "It helped.''

Her hand went away. She didn't say anything. He left the hack and went around to let her out. She stood a moment in the sunlight, a tall girl with her black hair reaching past her shoulders, looking steadily at him.

She said softly, "Think about what I said, Boot.'' Then she was gone, hurrying across to the little albino-eyed horse and the buggy. She got into the buggy and drove rapidly away, back toward the ferry. She really had moved back to the Bowman ranch, Lantry thought.

Jim Bill Dakin was still on the driver's seat of the hack. Boot stepped close and offered his hand. "Thanks, Jim Bill. Have you heard anything from Lute and Stafford since the other day?"

Jim Bill Dakin hesitated. His eyes were restless, avoiding Boot's friendly glance. He said at last, "I kind of dodged the truth when I met you up there close to Dead Man's Hollow, Boot. I hadn't seen Lute and Stafford that day. I took food to the cave they had been hiding in, but they weren't there. Under a big rock—the place we had picked out for such things— was a note from Lute, saying they would head back to the Cooksons, or cross the Arkansas line to the Ozarks. Said he and Stafford figured they'd better put distance between them and Fort Smith. The Cooksons would be my bet, but I don't like it. Too much bad influence there. Too many killers and robbers—and too many deputy marshals, trying to track those killers down."

Boot said firmly, "There's a lot of country to hide in, though. You have to say that for the Cooksons. Don't worry too much, Jim Bill. I'd almost bet that Lute and Stafford will be all right."

Old Jim Bill took a deep breath and shook his head sadly. "My boys didn't run so wild, Boot, until you left and stayed gone so long. I'll never forget how you sided them in Hemp Surate's place."

"I'd do it again, Jim Bill," Boot said, and watched Dakin drive on.

Taw had become impatient, his shod front hoof

pawing long streaks in the dust of the street where he was tied. Boot mounted and rode around to Garrison Street and swung down at the livery.

"Plenty of oats and water. And rub him down good," Boot told the hostler. "He appears to have kinks in his muscles from long standing. I'll be back after him in an hour."

The restaurant at the junction of the Van Buren Road and Garrison Street was crowded. Talk of the hanging that morning was rising strong. Boot slid onto a stool next to a man in a frayed tweed suit, who was reading a newspaper with huge block headlines:

## KILLER DIES OF STRANGULATION

Abundant subheads embellished the gory details:

### HANGMEN FAIL PITIFULLY
### HUNDREDS WATCH CRUEL GARROTING
### VICTIM BRAVE TO END
### MORE IN DUNGEON TO HANG

A flicker of anger stirred in Boot. "Why didn't you go watch it, fellow?"

The man in the tweed suit turned his head. He said in a clipped voice, "Thanks, but I'll take my stranglings second-hand."

Boot's appetite wasn't the best, but he ordered steak and ate, drank two cups of black coffee, then left the noisy restaurant and began deliberately easing the tension by walking along the street.

As he strolled he watched faces, hundreds of faces, trying to detect some traces of excitement or unease in the glances that touched his own. "When the crowds gather is the time to be on watch," the deputy marshal had said. And Boot Lantry had been watching the faces of men, young and old, for many hours.

A bay team hitched to a new Spaulding hack turned into the avenue from a side street and abruptly stopped.

"Lantry. I wonder if I could talk with you?"

It was Wes Cutler, on the seat of the hack alone.

Boot stopped and faced him. "Get it off your mind."

"Well, I mean, I want to discuss business with you. Now that . . . well, things have changed on the ranch, I'm wondering if there would be a chance of leasing some of the range from you?"

Boot stepped to the edge of the sidewalk. "So you've been snooping around our place? When?"

"I haven't! I'll swear I haven't!" Cutler said. "But one of my riders was looking for strays, and he met the part Indian woman—your brother's widow, I guess, on her way to Tahlequah. She told my rider the cattle would be sold."

Fury roiled inside Lantry. "If I ever find out one of your men stopped and badgered Lawana, I'll likely gut-shoot him, and you, too!"

"I'll swear, Lantry, I can't even talk to you in any kind of friendly way."

"No, you can't and you can't lease any of the Lantry holdings, or run cattle on the land—not as long as I can keep it under control, and that's likely to be for a hell of a long time, Cutler! Now drive on!"

The gall of the man was still raging through Boot

161

as he walked the sidewalks. Looking west toward the river, he saw Wes Cutler's hack whip left in the direction of the Federal courthouse. He guessed Cutler had some kind of business there.

Boot went to the livery and got Taw. He rode down toward Front Street, then stopped Taw and sat the saddle quietly, looking across the river into the hills of the Cherokee nation.

Sloan Vestal and the Hook Nine riders would be back at the ranch by now, he thought, saddling up fresh horses and getting the roundup under way.

Time dragged. Boot had a purpose in waiting and watching the river crossings and the roads from the Cherokee nation, but he found the waiting a difficult thing.

He thought once, I could relegate all this to U. S. deputy marshals, except that I have no proof. All I could do would be to point out confirmed enemies of the Lantry family, and to tell the marshals the thing that hit my mind when old Jeb's casket was opened and Tobe Jansen let loose such a tirade.

The promising rain clouds had blown away on the wings of the wind, and there was no sight of them except for a few blood-red banks settling over the face of the sinking sun. Boot rode past the Federal courtgrounds, looking for Wes Cutler or his bay team and hack. Cutler had not passed, returning across the river. But neither the hack and team nor Wes Cutler was in sight. Boot didn't see the hack and team until he rode to Hemp Surate's place on Smoky Row. They were standing among a half dozen or so bony hipshot horses at the tie-rail. Boot tied Taw to a willow a short distance away, and walked on.

He was beside the entrance to Surate's place when he heard Wes Cutler's voice inside.

"One of our neighbors was losing his life, and you fellows stayed holed up here like rats," Cutler was saying. "Has it ever occurred to you what people may think? You, Hemp. To outward appearances, you're running a border restaurant. Only those in the know realize the restaurant's a front for a blind tiger saloon. Don't either of you—my nephew Mace or you— know the importance of appearances now?"

"Don't start condemning me!" Hemp Surate growled. "Can you prove you was there?"

Silence stretched out tautly while Boot listened, then Mace Bracken's bitter, derisive voice took hold. "Why, sure, Uncle Wes could always prove he was at a given place at any given minute, couldn't you, Uncle Wes? Couldn't you?"

"Choke it down, Mace!" Cutler lashed at him. "If it ever becomes necessary, I'll swear I was in that crowd and watched Jeb Fentress choke to death."

"And it was a fearful thing, wasn't it, Uncle Wes? You couldn't hardly stand it, could you, now?"

"Shut your rotten mouth!"

Boot Lantry stepped inside, his boots echoing hollowly. He passed a couple of drunken Indians at one table, and three ragged and bearded oldsters at another. Boot had glimpsed them from where he had stopped outside, and he had realized instantly that their presence would block any definitely damaging statements Wes Cutler or the others would make. Boot had sensed that the argument might go on, but

163

there would have been only the innuendoes thrown out, the tantalizing phrases and half-thoughts that would never allow outsiders to grasp the whole truth. Boot stopped and looked at Cutler, and Surate and Mace Bracken. He thought, There was a time when Hook Nine riders would have dragged them out of here and seen that justice was done. Now, with Judge Parker heading the forces of justice, such things couldn't be done. About all Boot could hope for at this moment was to say something that might shake Cutler, Mace or Hemp.

"I'm looking for Sully Jansen," Boot said.

But it didn't appear to shake them. Wes Cutler and his nephew merely stared at Boot. Hemp Surate cursed.

"Hell, we don't try to ride herd on that snotnose fake," he said.

"Is that what Sully is, Hemp? A fake?"

"That's all he is!" Hemp Surate snarled. "A sniveling fake, toting a gun around, saying he's gonna kill somebody, that he knows this and he will do that, and all he ever does is sneak here and there through the brush like a smelly polecat. If it wasn't for the few errands I need him for, I'd freight his feet and dunk him for good in the river. I'd get rid of him."

"I suppose you would, at that," Boot said.

Hemp Surate's eyes got venomous. He took a slow drink from a tinted glass, and set the glass down and splayed his hands on the bar.

"I would. I'd get rid of him as a nuisance. Maybe even shoot him, the way you shot your brother and

164

your poor ol' pa!''

Surate's voice was like a knife slash in the pit of Boot Lantry's stomach.

"What did you say, Hemp?"

Hemp Surate leaned back and laughed, and Wes Cutler's big orbs swiveled around to him and stayed upon him. "Why, Hemp," Cutler said, "I'll swear, I never thought of it that way!"

"Me, neither, Uncle Wes," Mace Bracken sneered. "You're a genius of a man, that's what you are, Hemp! I'd never thought of the thing that way at all. That Lantry would kill his brother and pa!"

Boot was going toward the bar where Hemp Surate stood, but still Hemp wouldn't stop it.

"For their land and cattle," Hemp pressed. "Shot his own pa and brother down from ambush, just to get the property they had. Boot failed on the Verdigris, so he rode back and killed his own kin to get their property, and now he'd like to lay it all on someone like Sully Jansen, a poor little snotnose fake."

Boot hit Hemp Surate left handed just as the last word left his mouth. It was a slamming hook that caught Surate against the jaw.

He made an indrawn, whining racket, sucking breath past a tongue that clove to the roof of his mouth. Lantry followed the left with a smashing right.

Hemp Surate went down in a sliding roll, his body arcing up convulsively once before he struck the table legs where the two drunken Indians sat.

The Indians lurched to their feet, momentarily

bewildered, then one of them upended the table, tumbling it over Hemp. Both Indians hit the door at a run, giving vent to caterwauling whoops that echoed down the channel of the Poteau and bounced back from the bluffs below Cocaine Hill.

Boot spun around in time to see Mace Bracken cracking a whiskey bottle against the rough oak bar.

# Chapter Fifteen

Mace came at Boot with the jagged glass slashing, murderous intent spilling from his eyes. It flashed through Boot Lantry's brain that it was the second time in four days that he had unthinkingly given a deadly enemy the advantage of him. Boot had attended the hanging and the funeral unarmed, and had stayed in Fort Smith unarmed, feeling comparatively secure on this side of the Arkansas River.

Unarmed, but with reservations. That was Boot Lantry's situation now.

Because Boot had never gone wholly unarmed since his boyhood days, when he had fought Mace Bracken with slingshots in those bloody and hurting schoolground brawls. He knew an instant of self-flagellation, however, because he had not drawn his jackknife and held its open blade up his sleeve the moment he walked in.

It was plain that Mace Bracken wasn't going to

revert to shooting unless he had to. The moment Boot had stepped into Smoky Row, he was out of Arkansas, on the lawless Choctaw Strip between the Poteau River and the Arkansas line, where policemen from the city seldom if ever came. But the hanging had just taken place on the gibbet but a few hundred yards away, and deputy marshals were thick at the old court quarters. Mace wouldn't want any noise.

Mace was bent upon slashing Boot to sausage meat with the jagged portion of that broken bottle, and Wes Cutler was rising and suddenly urging him on.

"Make it stick, Mace! Kill him! Bleed him to death and I'll make it right with you, all the rest of your days!"

It was strange to Boot Lantry, but Mace Bracken suddenly stopped. "Would you, now, Uncle Wes?" he drawled.

It gave Boot time to whip out his knife and open it.

"Mace, watch out!" Wes Cutler said stridently. "Watch out!"

Somehow it made Lantry think of the time two years ago, when Mace had imbibed of too much rawgut and had pulled off such a blundering shot from the door.

Mace was not drunk enough that he would be ineffectual with that broken bottle, but he was still drunk enough that he couldn't fully weigh and judge things. He couldn't even judge that he was in any real danger from Boot Lantry's knife. Mace grinned with a show of his protruding upper teeth, and took time to brace himself against the bar with his left hand, just to pause and relish the thought of what he would do to Boot.

Lantry's right hand flashed back with the jack-knife and he hurled it. The knife was swift as an arrow, and as accurate as an arrow from a bow in a trained Indian hunter's hands.

The blade of the knife slithered soundlessly between the bones of Mace Bracken's left fist, pinning Mace to the bar.

Even the pain of it, at first, was possibly negligible, especially in Mace's half-drunken state. Then the pain came and the blood spurted, and Mace dropped the jagged portion of the bottle and began to moan.

Outside, above the sound of his moaning, the whooping of the two Indians blended like a panther's tremulous cry. Lantry turned his attention away from Mace and walked toward Wes Cutler.

"You want in on this little fling?"

"I didn't start it, Lantry! I'll swear I didn't!" His hand was lifting, easing toward the lapel of his coat.

Boot was almost against him. His fists were clenched.

"Go ahead and try to pull it, Cutler. It would do me good to knock your head right off your neck!"

Somewhere down near the river the roar of a pistol sounded. The wailing of the drunk Indians suddenly shut off. But shadows of men were darkening the door, and Boot glanced around to see four deputy marshals, headed by Travis Reaves, striding into the room.

They spread away on either side of the doorway the moment they entered. All four had guns in their hands. Their glances roved through the shadowy interior, passing over the limp form of Hemp Surate,

169

resting fleetingly on the three ragged oldsters at the table, none of whom had moved during the brawl.

"We ain't done a thing, marshals," one of the old scroungers said. "We ain't even drinkin' no hooch."

Travis Reaves was looking at Boot and Cutler then, and then along the bar at Mace.

Blood was forming a deep, dark pool, and Mace had stopped moaning and was wiggling the jack-knife, trying to pull it from where the blade was sunk deep in the wood of the bar. Travis Reaves stepped forward to help him, then said commandingly to the deputy marshals with him, "Get a bandage on that hand!"

Reaves then faced Cutler and Boot. "What's going on here?"

Boot answered him. "A fight. I came here looking for Sully Jansen. A little trouble broke out."

"A little trouble—and you've taken care of it?"

"I think so," Boot said.

He saw Reaves' eyes blink and then begin to darken with anger.

"Lantry, it seems to me you're out on the prod for trouble! I don't think we can afford to put up with much more of this. Who started this mess, anyhow?"

"Lantry did," Wes Cutler said. "He struck the first blow. I witnessed it—and so did two Indians and those three old fellows yonder."

Reaves turned. "Is that so, gentlemen?"

The oldsters looked at each other, pausing, dragging it out, surprised and happy to be asked their opinions by a U. S. deputy marshal, any of the men who ride for Parker. Then they nodded in unison and pointed at Boot.

"That big man slipped in and knocked Hemp thirty feet across this floor. Thirty damn feet at one lick!" one of the old-timers said.

Reaves blew his breath between his lips, making them tremble, raising sound like that of a chuffing stallion. "Now, boys," he chided, "I didn't ask for a windy. The damn room isn't even thirty feet long." He turned back to Boot. "Lantry, I think it would be a good thing if you go home. And maybe you ought to stay there a few days, until you cool off. Either that, or do some riding with us in the mountains. We're still combing the woods for the killer or killers of your brother and pa."

"I hope you find them, marshal," Boot said. "And thanks." He passed Reaves and the other deputy marshals and left the place without looking back.

A wolf pack in full cry streaked across the bottomlands beyond the Poteau, the echoes of their passing drifting back forlornly, rousing sadness in Boot as he waited at the Choctaw Wharf.

It was dark, but the moon was up. He heard the tread of boots and turned to see Travis Reaves and the other deputy marshals walking back toward the Federal courthouse. Behind them, on his hack, was Wes Cutler, driving on past the edge of the Coke Hill district toward the commercial ferry dock.

Boot was aboard the old Indian ferry, halfway across the river, carefully holding Taw's reins to keep the horse from spooking, when he heard the rattle and boom of pistol shots. Some drunk was having himself a wild splurge, shooting a pistol in a back alley along Front Street, Boot thought.

He wondered if the deputy marshals or Wes Cutler

would pause to investigate. Probably not. The sound of a blasting pistol was not alien or very unexpected along the river's edge in the western section of Old Fort Smith.

Later that night Boot stood alone in the big front room of the Hook Nine ranchhouse. He listened to the clock in the quietness, a deep soul-sickness inside him because Pa and No Fire had been so ruthlessly slain.

Sloan Vestal and the weary riders had long since fallen asleep in the bunkhouse, but Lantry, who had not slept in two nights, was still reluctant to seek his bed. He took his belt, holsters and gun from a peg on the wall and buckled them on to feel the pistol's familiar, comforting weight. Boot had felt naked all day long, even at the graveyard while services for Fentress were going on.

Boot sat for a long while with the gun on, staring into the few coals in the huge fireplace, thinking of the events of that day, weighing and judging them.

There was little doubt in his mind that Sully Jansen had killed Tice Bowman. The thought had darted with all its strange implications into Boot's mind the instant he had heard old Tobe Jansen's outburst.

It was the only logical explanation of the stand that Jeb Fentress had made. Sully was Jeb's illegitimate son by Ma Jansen, and Jeb loved him. When he had seen his son kill a man, Jeb had taken the blame on himself rather than let Sully face the hangman.

The picture was still hurtingly vivid in Boot's mind, the way old Jeb had looked at Sully, just before Jeb had plunged through the trap.

Somehow, Boot figured, Wes Cutler was involved. Just as Cutler hated the Lantrys for having better range than he had, it was possible Cutler had also held enmity toward Tice Bowman, a man with money who had come into the Territory, contacted the Cherokee National Council, and managed to secure leases for good range and water for his horses around Sulphur Springs. It was possible that Wes Cutler had hired Sully Jansen to kill Bowman, Lantry thought.

But thinking it and proving it were two different things. Boot felt there was only one way: to corner Sully Jansen and somehow make him talk. Boot was firm in his thinking that once a solution to Tice Bowman's death was reached, a clearer trail would open and lead straight to the men who had killed Pa and No Fire.

Lantry figured Mace Bracken and Hemp Surate were involved in that. But who else had sided them? Boot could not clearly see how Sully Jansen, even fast as Sully had ridden away from him that day on Garrison Creek, could have joined a group of killers and gone to the Hook Nine ranch to indulge in prearranged rifle fire from ambush. His only weapon at the time Boot had met Sully was that .38 special pistol on its .45 frame.

Lantry rose and went to his bedroom, a persistent thought that had ridden his mind for several days still dogging him: Who had sent that message by Indian runner, requesting in all urgency that Boot hurry home?

There were some frustrating, puzzling tangents to everything that had happened here, Lantry thought.

He took off his belt and gun, undressed and sought his bed. But the frustration and the loneliness were still in him. There was seemingly no end to the way things and people could change in a few short months, let alone two full years. Sully Jansen had always been a little arrogant and unruly, but Lantry had never marked him as a kid that would go wholly bad. Lantry had retained faith in Sully, just as he had held to faith in old Jim Bill Dakin's two boys, Stafford and Lute.

And now take them, for instance. Even old Jim Bill had admitted to Lantry that he feared his sons had lied to him. It must be getting so that boys from good families were rebelling against their raising, violating all the rules of good conduct and fairness. It must be the reason so many young men were being arrested in the Territory, and taken to Fort Smith and hanged.

Boot sought his bed at last, but sleep was a long time in coming. He listened to the soughing sound of wind in the sycamore trees and the whisper of loneliness was there. An owl hooted sonorously at the edge of Grassy Lake, and in that sound also were suggestions of loneliness and despair.

He stretched, trying to ease his tension, lying wide-eyed in the darkness of the room. And it was strange, but mingling with all the lonely night sounds was the remembered sound of Sue Bowman's voice.

"Women have to take a stand against violence," Sue had said, and there had been tears in her blue eyes.

Suddenly Sue Bowman's face with the intriguing blue eyes appeared to be looking down at him from the darkened ceiling. It was odd, Boot Lantry thought, that the face now haunting him in the night was not that of Ina Jansen. Ina was not there at all. . . .

He roused at daylight and hurriedly dressed. Through the window he saw Sloan Vestal and the Hook Nine riders moving out across the rangeland, all set for another day of hard riding on the roundup in the brushy hills.

Boot cooked himself a breakfast of bacon and scrambled eggs, chasing the food with strong black coffee. Later he shaved, buckled on his gun, and went outside to stare eastward, in the direction of Fort Smith.

Tendrils of mist weaved their way up from Grassy Lake and disappeared with the approach of sunlight. Out of the mist along the Fort Smith road a lone rider appeared, traveling at breakneck speed toward the Hook Nine ranch.

Boot watched the rider with a faint unease, hearing the drumming of hoofbeats steadily drawing closer. Even the creaking of the saddle was audible as the rider neared, and the bellowslike breathing of the goaded horse revealed how hard and fast the mount had been ridden.

Then Boot recognized old Jim Bill Dakin. He heaved his horse to a sliding halt.

"Boot! Half the deputy marshals in town are coming here! They're due here any minute, circling around the south side of Grassy Lake."

"Get down and rest yourself, Jim Bill. You look all worked up."

The old man swung down, but stopped at the yard gate, breathing heavily and leaning forward, his sharp gaze reaching at Boot.

"You'll think worked up, if you don't listen to what I tell you!" the old man blurted. "You won't have a ghost of a chance if them lawmen nab you. Wes Cutler was killed last night!"

# Chapter Sixteen

Boot walked down the porch steps. "What time? Where?"

"He was found dead on Front Street, with four slugs in his back. Wasn't found until almost daylight this morning, but a deputy marshal told me a doctor stated Wes had been dead at least all night."

"Does anyone know who did it?"

"That's what I'm tryin' to tell you, Boot! Mace Bracken swore he saw you kill his uncle, right after Cutler had left Hemp Surate's place last night!"

Boot remembered the gunshots he had heard from Front Street. "Mace Bracken's a liar! If he saw his uncle killed, why didn't he report it right after it happened?"

"Well, that's what the marshals asked Mace, but he had his answer ready for them. Said you slugged him with a gun and took him across the Arkansas. Told the marshals you dragged him most of the way through these bottoms, and Mace sure looked it, too. When I saw him, his new suit was ruined, he had mud and sand all over him, and his hat and even his shoes was gone. Mace said you shoved him into the muck of Grassy Lake and left him for dead, but that he come to and got back to town on foot."

"Do you believe I did that killing, Jim Bill?"

"No!" the old man almost shouted. "But what I'm tellin' you is that a case is being built against you that can take you right to the gallows. You're gonna have to run for your life."

"I can't run from something like this, Jim Bill. I'm innocent."

"Innocent? So was Jeb Fentress, you say. I heard you tell Miss Bowman that Jeb didn't kill her pa. But Jeb Fentress died on the gallows, and so will you if you don't start riding, and pretty damn quick! Your only chance is to get on a fast horse and light out! It's the only way you have a chance of staying free and searching for the killers of your brother and your pa, or of maybe proving that the men you suspect are guilty. Stay gone until the truth about Wes Cutler's killing leaks out."

"Running from something doesn't come natural with me."

"I know that, too," Jim Bill said. "But a fast ride now is your only hope."

Boot saw a dust cloud forming on the horizon, like a whirlwind moving fast through scattered timber just west of Grassy Lake. In the dust appeared the shapes of horses and riders, moving swiftly toward the ranch.

"Yonder they come, Boot!" Jim Bill Dakin said.

178

"Time's runnin' out on you. Saddle up and ride. Head for the hills. Somewhere in the Cooksons you'll contact Lute and Stafford. You boys may find somethin' in common that will help to clear up these things."

Boot Lantry barely heard him. He kept staring at the dust and the approaching deputy marshals, and in his mind was a vision of two stark and shocking things: the dungeon jail, and old Jeb Fentress dying on the gallows.

Boot Lantry could easily die there too.

"All right, Jim Bill," Boot said. "I'll be traveling." He stepped forward quickly and gripped old Jim Bill's hand. "And thanks."

Boot's long stride carried him to the corral where he had left Taw. He whistled to the black, and swiftly bridled and saddled him.

By the time he had opened the corral gate, led Taw through and mounted, the cavalcade of deputy marshals was less than two hundred yards away.

It was a credit to them, Boot Lantry thought, that they didn't start using rifles. They swerved their mounts, striving to short-cut him as he circled past the corrals, but none of them was shooting. He guessed they were bent upon circling him, herding him in and capturing him without gunplay. Boot leaned forward over the horn of his saddle, his heels pressing Taw's sides. The big horse sailed over a ditch like a winged Pegasus and thundered across a stretch of alkali terrain, straining for his utmost speed.

Boot twisted in the saddle and saw that the deputy marshals were spreading, possibly thinking he

179

might circle back, once he struck the shelter of the forest. But that was strategy which Lantry's quick mind had already toyed with and rejected. He knew that his only chance of avoiding capture rested in Taw's incredible speed and endurance over a distance of many miles. He sent Taw like a black streak, crashing straight into the first belts of woods and through them, on toward the uplift of rugged hills.

Boot looked back again and saw the scattered cavalcade burst from the woods behind him. It was almost unbelievable, but it was apparent that the deputy marshals had gained on him. They were riding some swift quarter horses, Boot thought.

Boot leaned forward, his broad hat off, his black hair raked by the branches of the trees and wildly wind-tossed, making him look like one of Pike's Indian raiders on a charge during the Civil War.

"Taw!" he said into the big horse's flattened ears.

That was all he said, a firm but affectionate master's plea to loyal horseflesh. Taw's nostrils flared, and he pushed his head out almost level with his neck and shoulders, straight into the rush of wind.

The flicker of a smile crossed Boot Lantry's face as he felt the extra burst of speed. The sound of Taw's hoofs was muted as he raced across a natural meadow, then dipped down for the crossing of Garrison Creek.

There were two main routes northward past Old Payne's Mountain—the one between the Jansen place and the Bowman ranch and the other up Garrison Creek Hollow. As Taw clattered across the creek and up the north bank, Lantry swiftly debated, then decided to take the Garrison Creek route.

He knew he could send Taw scrambling up the rough, timbered face of Payne's Mountain itself, but that course might allow the deputy marshals to split and outride him on the lowland routes, and possibly intercept him at the interlacing of roads and trails northwest of Czarnikow Creek, a meandering stream that tumbled down out of several small branches on the northern slopes of the hills.

He reined to the left and gave Taw his head through the forested region. Behind him he heard the clamor of iron-shod hoofs on rocks as the deputy marshals crossed the creek. A rise in the terrain loomed ahead, and when Taw crested it, Boot looked back again.

No riders were in sight. Boot's sharp turn up the course of the creek bank had temporarily made them override his trail. He had gained on them. He felt Taw's unfaltering strength under him and knew it was enough gain to allow him to feel comparatively safe.

But he didn't check Taw's tremendous burst of speed. Not yet. Boot waited until he saw, up near the mouth of Sulphur Springs Hollow, the front veranda of the Bowman ranch. Then he stopped Taw a moment to listen. Far behind him he could hear horses and riders tearing through the underbrush, but he knew they would never be able to overtake him now.

He sent Taw on at a reaching lope, passing the Bowman place and turning gradually northward again.

He struck the same road he had traveled the day he

had met Jim Bill Dakin and Sully Jansen. The road hugged the east side of the hollow, winding in switchback turns over ancient rock culverts where freight wagons had been rolling into the Territory for almost fifty years. Then, realizing he could easily meet someone who might detain him, Boot sent Taw off on a side trail that carried him high atop the bluffs beside the stream.

Long pools of blue water shone below him. A few cows wearing the Hook Nine brand were shambling down the opposite slope to drink. Boot slowed Taw to watch them, his mind locked in memories of Pa and No Fire, reliving the good days that used to be.

He was riding along, tired and lax in his saddle, when the cold breath of warning suddenly hit him. He tensed and abruptly reined Taw from the trail, but his acute sense of sound and movement had jolted him from his reverie too late.

He heard the rifle shot and the screaming of the bullet as it peeled bark from a post oak tree scant inches from his head. He ducked instinctively, then lifted his head and saw Hemp Surate and two of Wes Cutler's young riders standing on the edge of a cliff about fifty yards away.

Boot had time to think that Hemp Surate had somehow guessed which direction Boot would take if he fled from the deputy marshals. Or perhaps Hemp had other Cutler riders blocking the road around Payne's Mountain on the east side, too. But those were the only thoughts that Boot had time for. He never heard the sound of the second shot. The bullet preceded the gunsound, striking his head with an explosive burst of pain.

Taw reared, his front hoofs pawing, dancing sideward and teetering right at the edge of the sheer bluffs as Boot reeled in the saddle. Then, as another rifle shot sounded and a bullet slammed into the pommel of the saddle, the big horse bolted.

Boot Lantry fell.

Vague consciousness returned to him just as he tumbled from the saddle. He groped wildly, but he was powerless to halt his downward plunge. His body had done a complete somersault when he left the saddle. He crashed feet-first through the tangled branches of cedar saplings that grew out from the crevices in the rocks.

He felt a cushioning splash of coolness, and knew he had broken the surface of Garrison Creek. He went under in the long, deep pool, then fought his way to the top. The water was cooling the sudden fever in him, but his senses were still badly blurred. He started swimming, angling toward the dark outline of trees along the shore.

He struggled against the agonizing pain in his head that was threatening to craze him. At last he straightened, and felt the rough and rock-jumbled bottom of the pool under his boots. His hands clawed out, and his fingers clamped around an overhanging branch of a sycamore tree.

Boot steadied himself, gasping for more air, and finally pulled his drenched and shivering body up to the grassy shore of the stream. He stretched out there for a moment, exhausted, chilled to the bone.

He felt warm blood gushing down the side of his face and knew he needed to stop it, but the thought of Hemp Surate and those young thugs who had ridden for Cutler was gnawing at his mind.

Boot felt for his gun, and found to his relief that he hadn't lost it. But when he pulled it from the snug scabbard and looked at it, he saw how it was drenched with water, and he feared it was temporarily useless. Still thinking of Hemp Surate and the men that had ridden for Cutler, Boot dragged himself cautiously into a matting of sourvines and hid.

He waited, striving to hold his breath to listen, but it was several minutes before he heard anything. When he did it was nearby, a thunderous sound, the pounding of many hoofbeats going away up the hollow. Evidently they figured they had killed him, Boot thought. The sound of their horses finally dwindled and faded away.

Boot crawled from the tangle and rose dizzily to his feet. He felt above his right ear, and told himself the bullet had merely creased him, but the wound was deep and long and still spurting blood.

He felt his strength draining out, and knew he had to stop that blood.

He got his wet shirt off and twisted it into a bandage. He tied it around his head. He started walking, and there was only one thought in his brain. Sue Bowman's Circle S Ranch was less than two miles down the stream. It was even closer than that if he could climb the rocky hogback that jutted out north and south along the western portion of the ridge.

He decided to attempt the climb, and realized an instant later it was a good thing he had made that decision. The close-packed cordon of mounted U. S. deputy marshals rounded a turn in the road below and swept past, traveling swiftly north.

The fact that he had temporarily forgotten the lawmen who were pursuing him made Boot realize fully the seriousness of the wound in his head.

He stood a moment with a growing bewilderment upon him, then whistled urgently for Taw. The effort of whistling sent nausea surging through him, and he knew by his shortened breathing that shock was grabbing him in its relentless clutch.

At last he saw his horse, but it was through a vast, swirling void of clammy sickness. Before Taw reached him Boot was staggering and falling again, dropping through a garish world of darkness that enveloped him like a pall. . . .

# Chapter Seventeen

He became vaguely aware of the sound of nearby voices, then opened his eyes and saw the shadow of someone stooping, holding a lighted lantern close to his eyes. The voices were barely murmuring. It was low and cautious discussion, and the voices seemed familiar. Boot tried to rise, but when he did the shapes of two men became erratic, and their talk was a mere droning, like sound that was coming from a long way off.

"Lute! Stafford!" Boot said.

There was almost instant silence, then the familiar voice of Lute Dakin sounded close to Lantry's ear. "Boot, pardner, you recognize us! You're gonna be all right!"

Boot lay back, breathing heavily. "Your pa told me you boys had left these hills."

Stafford Dakin spoke next. "We didn't want Pa taking the risk of toting food to us. We wrote that note and left it, and watched from the brush when he picked it up. We never really aimed to leave."

Blood was still coursing from the wound in Boot Lantry's head. He could feel the warm, viscid flow of it, writhing down his neck. He could feel himself getting weaker, too, and knew he had to talk fast.

"You fellows listen! Right over the slope is the Bowman horse ranch. If I'm not imposing, if you can afford to go there, maybe I could get to clean bandages, some kind of medicine, some . . ."

He didn't get it finished. Another black pall of sickness blotted consciousness out.

For an interminable time he seemed to be floating through a stark world that held neither light nor darkness. Then through that realm of nothingness a wall of encroaching mist appeared and vanished and it was day.

It was daylight. He was lying on a bed under clean white sheets, beside an open window. Dimly, he saw Sue Bowman's face. She was close to the bed, bending over him. Behind her stood Lute and Stafford, their thin faces tense, their eyes alert and concerned.

Boot tried to lift his head, but couldn't. He lay back with a vast lassitude upon him, looking up at Sue.

"How bad was I hit?"

She rested a hand against the thick bandage around his head. "You lost a lot of blood. Are you hungry, Boot?"

"Yep." He forced a smile. "Yep, I believe I am."

"Good." She flashed a bright smile at him and left.

Stafford and Lute Dakin moved up close to the bed.

"Thanks, Lute . . . Stafford," Boot murmured. "I won't forget."

Lute and Stafford grinned with gaunt, hungry faces. Both were worn down, weary, disheveled from lack of sleep. For a moment they merely looked at Boot without talking, then Lute said, "You talked some crazy stuff about Sully Jansen. Did that foxy weakling shoot you down?"

"No. It was Hemp Surate. Hemp had some of Wes Cutler's hired gunslingers with him. No, I just had Sully on my mind, that was all."

"Why?" Stafford Dakin asked.

Boot told them, speaking quietly. The Dakin brothers looked at each other. Lute said, "While you're resting up here, getting yourself back in condition, Staff and me are gonna be scouting around. If we can nab Sully, we'll bring him to you. We'll all just haul off and wring the truth out of him."

"The woods are full of deputy marshals, Lute," Boot warned.

Lute forced another grin. "Well, we're tired of hiding like timber wolves, me and Staff are. I guess, sooner or later, we'll go in and give ourselves up to the law." Lute paused, wiping a gnarled, thin hand across his forehead. "Boot?"

"Yes?"

"We know a little about Sully, and about Hemp Surate and Mace Bracken. You see, me and Staff got pretty desperate, after being forced to leave on account of that trumped up cattle-stealing charge. But later Hemp and Mace contacted us, and said they'd like for us to forget the trouble, and maybe join them in a deal that Wes Cutler had cooked up."

"I see." Boot looked at the brothers steadily. "So

you took them up?"

"Well, not all at once," Stafford Dakin cut in. "Not until they explained it all." He paused and grinned crookedly. "And it was a pretty neat plan, I'll tell you."

"Yeah," Lute hurried on. "Neat. Wes Cutler had a plan to rustle Hook Nine blind, and scare your pa and No Fire out of the country. What Hemp and Mace wanted me and Staff to do was accept them stolen cattle from Hook Nine and run them up to a thieving ring in the Pottawatomie Indian country— Old Pott Country, the folks up there call it. Me and Staff was hard up for money, and we did take up that first batch of beef. We wanted to tell you that."

"Is that all you fellows have done in the way of violating the law?"

Stafford nodded. "That about wraps it up. And we didn't mean much harm that time, Boot. You see, when we found out a plan was cooking to ruin Hook Nine, me and Lute fell in with it to find out all we could. We aimed to help your folks. We aimed to make it right, about that one batch of stolen beef."

Boot kept looking at them. "I'll call things square now. Don't think any more about it. And stay away from town. When I get things cleared up, I'd like to have you fellows with me, splitting the breeze after wild cattle up on the Verdigris."

"We're gonna have to clear our names first, Boot. We've been accused of a lot of things we never done, but it was wrong to ever side Hemp, Mace and Cutler at all. I figure they shaped up the killing of No Fire and your pa."

Sue Bowman returned to the room, carrying a

bowl of warm broth. "No more talking," she said firmly. "Use your strength to eat this. It's very good."

She smiled and sat on the edge of the bed beside him. Lute and Stafford Dakin lifted hands to Boot in gestures of farewell, and tiptoed out of the house. Boot turned his head to look through the open window. He could see the wooded pitch of the mountains beyond the cluster of cedar log corrals. Presently his gaze picked up Lute and Stafford, riding their bony horses through the timber toward the Jansen place.

"Here!" Sue Bowman commanded. "You eat this, now."

She smiled as she began to feed him. Boot watched her face as he ate. Sunlight through the window drew a spangled luster from her thick, black hair. In her eyes was a steady compassion, and the same strong feeling showed at the corners of her full lips.

The warm broth was pleasant against his stomach, sending feelers of renewed strength coursing along his veins. He emptied the bowl and watched Sue drop the spoon into it with a lively clatter. She rose and stood, briefly smiling down at him.

"Sue."

She turned back to him.

"Sue, what does Mace Bracken mean to you?"

He felt instantly that he shouldn't have asked it. She looked past him through the window, her glance sweeping over the tall hills, and there was disturbance in her eyes.

"Well, I was attracted to him for a while, even friendly with him. He was so thoughtful and courteous, and seemed such a gentleman during

Dad's funeral. But after his outburst on the street, his cursing and violence and his obvious hatred of the Lantry family, I knew at once that a man like him could never mean anything to me. Not anything. I despise people who nurse hatreds, who thrive on contentions. I . . . I think, in a way, I almost despise you, Boot, because of the things I sense you are capable of doing. It wouldn't be very difficult for you to kill a man, would it?''

Lantry forced himself to a sitting position on the bed, bracing himself with shaky arms. Dizziness consumed him, but it was not a lasting thing. He looked intently at Sue Bowman.

"You're wrong," Boot said. "It's never been an easy thing for me to pull the trigger on a human being, not even when my own life was threatened. But self-preservation is a strong instinct. And I was raised in this frontier country with certain firm principles drilled into me—that when men threatened my life, I'd better do something about it. That when enemies killed my friends, or members of my family, I'd better do something about that, too."

She stood slightly in profile to him. He felt the brilliant, sideward impact of her gaze.

"So you're going to do something about it?" she queried.

Boot dipped his head. "If I expect to live in the Indian Territory, to build a ranch, to become a leader with any influence, then I have to handle my problems. It's the only way."

She lifted her face and stood looking out through the upper panes of the window. He sensed that tears were close to the surface of her eyes.

192

"You're a man of good education, Boot. I realized that the second time I met you. Didn't you attend school in the East?"

"In the Carolinas, the old Cherokee country," he said.

"I thought so. Didn't they teach any subjects on the law, the humanities, about culture?"

"I was taught many things," Boot replied, "but some have never been of much use to me. Maybe for a circuit judge or store clerk, or polished Territorial lawyer, but not for a man that makes his living on the range. The learning that counts here is the kind that helps you sit a bucking horse, or a fast cow pony, or how to use a rope, knife or gun. I found that out."

"You could turn your problem over to United States marshals. You know you could."

Boot nodded. "Sure. But even if Mace Bracken and Hemp Surate are found guilty and hanged, there are their cohorts, the thugs Wes Cutler hired. They're the kind of ruthless, back-shooting killers that the marshals can't touch without more proof. And those are the kind that would dog me, no matter where I rode or walked. Because they would figure I was weak, just because I turned the job over to marshals. It's always the weak ones that the wolf packs jump."

Sue Bowman's strong hands locked and unlocked nervously. "If that kind of thinking continues, Boot, then when will the country ever be safe for persons who despise the law of the gun?"

Boot lay back. "Maybe after Judge Parker's hanging court has eliminated most of the killers," he said. "But that time is not yet."

Sue left the room hurriedly, saying over her

shoulder, "Get some rest." Her voice was hurt, bitter. "In a few days you'll be able to ride out and show people everywhere, all over the Indian nations, that no one ever crosses a Lantry without paying the price!"

She was beyond the doorway when Boot's urgent voice stopped her.

"Sue, where is my gun?"

He heard no answer from her, and he rose upright again and looked searchingly about the room. His eyes were still searching when he heard Sue's returning footsteps. She was carrying his cartridge-studded gunbelt, holster and pistol. She came close and hung them on the post of the bed.

"There you are," she said. Her face was expressionless. "Now you're fixed right up. The Dakin boys cleaned and oiled the unsightly weapon. Put your hands on it! Make a vow again to your ancestral clans that the so-called wolf packs that try to challenge you, or cross the Lantry pathway, will have their lives ended with powder and lead!"

Sue Bowman choked and spun about and left him there. He listened to the sound of her footsteps; the tapping of her heels was like a soft drumbeat of finality, signaling for Boot the end of a dream that was being stopped almost as soon as it had begun.

He slept, and when he roused again it was nighttime and the wolf pack was there.

# Chapter Eighteen

He first heard the clumping of heavy boots in the front room, then the sound of Mace Bracken cursing. Mingled with Mace's cursing was the high-pitched and demanding voice of Hemp Surate.

"We know he's here! After we sidetracked them deputy marshals, we rode back to that water hole to make sure Lantry was dead. He wasn't there, but we followed the trail of blood! By God, sister, I'm warning you! You'd better move aside and let us look!"

"I won't do it!" Sue Bowman cried. "You get out of here! All of you! I've never heard such foul-mouthed men in all my life—Mr. Bracken, in all decency, won't you stop this terrible thing?"

Mace laughed. Again it was like the sound of pebbles dropping into a still, dark pool. It was the way Mace's laughter always was when he had a killing yen.

"You step aside," Mace hurled at her. "It ain't gonna take but one close and fast shot for me to do Lantry in."

"No!" Sue's voice had a panicked note. "I won't let you do it! He's wounded, helpless. I'll never let you kill him. You'll have to kill me first."

Boot eased back the quilts, lifted himself and reached to grip the butt of his pistol. He heard the sickening smack of flesh against flesh, followed by the sound of Sue's stifled scream.

Boot forced himself to stand. The room tilted crazily and a sledge-hammering sickness pounded in his head. He fought it and stayed on his feet, feeling the palpable weakness and the leaden weight of his .45.

He heard another slap, and more cursing, and Hemp Surate's merciless voice. "We'll beat you to death and leave you here if you don't get out of our way."

"No, we won't do that, Hemp." That was Mace again. "I figure she'll make a right lively little ridin' partner. We'll take her along on the trail after we've finished Lantry."

Mace laughed again, then cut it off abruptly. Lantry heard a sudden pounding, and Sue's whimpering cry, and knew that Mace had struck her with his fist.

Boot lifted his face in the darkness and breathed a prayer. He moved away from the bed, his whole attention focused upon the faint beam of candlelight that squeezed between the tiny slit up and down from the latch of the door. His dizziness gradually faded. He was thinking clearly now.

The only trouble was, he could barely lift the big gun and steady it. He thumbed back the hammer. There was no real strategy in his mind; time did not permit it. He heard another cry from Sue Bowman, and this time it was filled with terror. They had gone beyond just striking her.

He reached the door and groped for the knob, and somehow out of his desperation and fury a renewed portion of strength was born. He wrenched open the door and slammed it against the wall behind him, and stepped through facing them.

Boot's eyes took in the whole stark picture at one glance. He recognized four of the young riders who had been with Cutler on Garrison Creek, that day Boot had spooked the herd. He saw Hemp Surate, standing with a wide-legged stance in the center of the room. Just beyond Hemp were Mace Bracken and Sue Bowman. Mace had his left arm locked about her waist, straining her against him, holding her helpless like a shield.

Boot saw the eyes of every man start bulging. They had believed Boot Lantry was helpless. Boot's lips twisted. His glance, dark with fury, whipped from Hemp to Mace.

There was no time for talk, because hands were streaking for gun butts. There was only a small portion of Mace's body that was visible—his face, which Boot dared not shoot at, because Sue Bowman was a tall girl, and her own face was too close to the line of fire.

Then Mace's right boot slid sideward a little, going out past Sue's slipper. Boot's pistol slanted downward. The concussion from the shot thundered around the walls of the room and slammed against the ceiling. Mace Bracken sucked in his breath and held it, his face becoming a garish, swollen mask. He went far sideward, reaching down as if to halt the searing impact of the bullet through the flesh and blood and bones of his lower leg.

Boot ducked behind the facing of the door as guns launched their simultaneous bombardment of lead at him. He heard the bullets ripping splinters from the facing, and the sound of their weird squall and whine as they ricocheted. He dropped down to his knees and began to return the fire from a point about two feet above the floor.

He killed Hemp Surate with a heart shot, then turned his gun on Mace.

Bracken was still holding Sue with his left arm and trying to steady his pistol with his right, but Sue was fighting him. And there was pain still spilling from Mace's eyes; he was still attempting to twist down, to stop the bone-crushing agony in his leg. He was a man of many impulses, twitching like a fly in a web.

Cutler's young thugs suddenly wheeled and bolted for the front door, their smoking six-shooters dangling in their hands.

"I heard horses!" one of them shouted. "Somebody's coming Mace!"

Mace Bracken groaned. His impulses were still drawn in two directions. Boot saw that he was striving to steady his gun, but evidently the pain in his leg and Sue Bowman's struggles and clawing fingers would not let him do it.

Boot fanned the hammer of his .45, moved by a touch of mercy. He shot Mace Brakcen squarely between the eyes.

There was a brief time when the room was empty except for Sue and Boot and the dead bodies of Mace and Hemp. Sue glanced down at Bracken and cringed, then rushed across the room and knelt in front of Boot. He saw her shaking hands reaching out, and felt them touch his face.

"Boot, are you hurt?"

"Not a bit."

Her eyes were great wide pools of horror. "Boot, forgive me for what I said to you." She still held his face, but her head turned, and she looked at the bodies of Mace and Hemp. She shuddered. "They were like . . . like beasts, weren't they?"

She was still kneeling in front of Boot, her face pressing down against his shoulder, crying convulsively when three deputy marshals stepped in. One of them was Travis Reaves.

Behind them, his run-over boots making a cautious, uncertain sound, was Sully Jansen. Following Sully were Stafford and Lute.

"We know what it is to run, to be chased and hounded," Lute Dakin said. "So we figured we'd better just bring Sully and the officers in on this. Looks to me like you've fought a war."

Lute and Stafford got Boot into a comfortable chair, and arranged a chair for Sue. The deputy marshals examined the two bodies, then picked up the guns which Mace and Hemp had dropped, and carefully examined them. They broke out the cylinders of the guns, taking count of the shots that had been fired. They examined Boot's gun the same way.

"You ought to pinch yourself, Lantry, to see if you're still alive," Reaves said.

He turned and approached Sue Bowman. "Tell us about it. Everything. Exactly how it was."

Sue told them. Travis dipped his head, then gestured at Sully. "Now, kid, you say your little piece to Lantry," the marshal said.

Sully's face had lost all semblance of arrogance or defiance. He looked pale and weak.

"I've done things wrong, but not any killing," he said. "I helped Mace and Hemp and some of Cutler's riders steal Hook Nine cattle, and I reckon I'll pay the price for that. But I never killed anyone."

Boot's questioning stare held upon him. "You didn't kill Tice Bowman?"

"No," Sully said. "The day Bowman was killed, Mace borrowed my little pony. I didn't know what he wanted it for. I waited out in the woods, then I heard some pistol shots, and Mace didn't come back with my horse. I left the woods and saw my pony standing close to a dead man."

Sully stopped a moment and looked down at Mace's body, then hurried on with it.

"Like I say, Bowman was dead, and there was this pretty pistol—the .38 on a .45 frame—and Mace was nowhere in sight. I picked up the pistol and was standing there holding it when Jeb Fentress, the Hook Nine foreman, rode out of the brush and saw me. I was shook up some, and I jumped on my pony and left. I guess I wasn't thinking straight. I wasn't certain for a long time that Jeb Fentress hadn't killed Tice Bowman. I had heard Mace and Hemp talk some, about how maybe the Lantrys wouldn't like for Bowman to start a ranch close to the old Sulphur Springs. But then one night Mace was drinking heavy, and he told me he killed Bowman. He just laughed and winked, and said he'd have a free hand with Bowman's daughter. I ought to have done some talking then, but I guess I was scared to. I was kind of tangled up with Hemp and Mace, and they promised me I'd get some money if I'd keep my mouth shut and do some cattle stealing for them. I know I'll pay for all that. . . .''

"Stop rambling, Sully," Boot said. "Do you know who killed my brother and pa?"

Sully licked dry lips. "It was Hemp and Mace that done the shooting. Two of Cutler's riders was with them, but I didn't see them shoot. They didn't have any rifles, as far as I could tell. I saw it all. I was in a rage at you, after you grabbed me and took my gun on Garrison Creek. I was snooping about the ranch, stewing and fretting over that, but I wouldn't 've done anything. I think, from the way Hemp and Mace talked while I hid and listened, they hoped you would be at the corrals with your brother and your pa that evening. They wanted to take all the Lantrys at one lick. It was Hemp that sent word for you to come back from the Verdigris. I saw him write out that note, and him and Wes Cutler and Mace all laughed about that, too. Cutler was ramrodding a lot of dirty work around these parts, and I've got to come clean and tell you that my sister Ina knowed it. She sure knowed it! She's a pretender, like my damned ol' fake of a pa! Sometimes I wouldn't doubt a bit that she wanted all the Lantrys out of the way, just like Cutler and Mace and Hemp did, but I reckon nobody

201

wanted it more than Hemp and Mace. They told me they never got over the way you bested them, when you sided the Dakin boys two years ago.''

Boot leaned back in his chair. "Who killed Wes Cutler, Sully?"

Sully's glance dropped down to the body of Mace Bracken. "He done it. I know he did, because his uncle had been trying to keep him sober, always badgering him, and not shelling out the money like he once had. I know . . .''

The voice of Travis Reaves took it up. "We're pretty certain about that too, Lantry. Mace looked too smug, too satisfied, when I sent deputy marshals out after you. So I began to question him.''

Lantry's senses quickened. "What did you find out?"

"Well, I forced Mace to allow a doctor to examine him, and the doctor said there was no sign on Mace's head that he had been hit with a gun. I got the idea Mace was making up that yarn about you forcing him across into the Territory and leaving him in the muck of the lake. I warned Mace to stay close around town, that I'd want to talk to him more later. I guess he figured the jig was up, and that he'd better start high-tailing, but evidently he and Hemp wanted to make sure they got you first.'' Travis stopped talking and gestured to his companions. "Let's get 'em out of here. They won't have to wait for the hangman. Not these two.''

Boot looked at Sully Jansen and knew Sully was finished with his talk. It was all right. Boot Lantry didn't want any more talk, any more post-mortems. A phase of Boot Lantry's life, of his experiences, was

202

done. He looked at Sue Bowman, and she looked back at him. A new day would dawn for them.

"Thanks, Sully," Boot said.


Indian Joe was over his sickness, but the world was a sad and dreary and forlorn place to be.

He squatted on the slope with his fat wife, digging roots beside her in a dense thicket of sassafras above a narrow forest trail that led away from the Bowman horse ranch and wound up to the source of Sulphur Springs.

Joe's wife could always find good places to dig for roots, he thought. He looked at her, wishing she would talk to him, or offer him a good dip of snuff like she used to do. Indian Joe's wife hadn't spoken one word to him, or offered him that snuff box, since his last abandoned binge on Fort Smith hooch.

Sound of talk and footsteps on the trail alerted Indian Joe. He peered around the edge of the sassafras thicket and saw Boot Lantry and the pretty dark-haired girl from the Bowman ranch.

As Indian Joe watched, they stopped on the trail and stood close to each other, holding hands. Joe listened to their talk, straining his ears for every word, and finally the tracing of a smile built on his face.

Indian Joe scurried happily around the thicket and stopped behind his wife. He touched her shoulder, then flinched slightly as she spun around.

Her sharp tongue struck at him. "What you want, ol' man?"

Indian Joe throttled his unease and gave her his

warmest smile. He groped for the words he had heard Boot Lantry say. He did his best to repeat them. "Me . . . you . . . love!" Indian Joe said.

His fat wife read his lips, and she dropped her digging fork and stared.

Indian Joe recalled another phrase, and he said it. "You go me up Verdigris?"

"Joe!" his wife said. "We can't go up Verdigris. But me . . . you . . . love!" Her voice was soft and her eyes were as warm as summer sunbeams, shining bright on Old Payne Hill.

# THE NEWEST ADVENTURES AND ESCAPADES OF BOLT
## by Cort Martin

**#11: THE LAST BORDELLO**                    (1224, $2.25)

A working girl in Angel's camp doesn't stand a chance—unless Jared Bolt takes up arms to bring a little peace to the town . . . and discovers that the trouble is caused by a woman who used to do the same!

**#12: THE HANGTOWN HARLOTS**                    (1275, $2.25)

When the miners come to town, the local girls are used to having wild parties, but events are turning ugly . . . and murderous. Jared Bolt knows the trade of tricking better than anyone, though, and is always the first to come to a lady in need . . .

**#13: MONTANA MISTRESS**                    (1316, $2.25)

Roland Cameron owns the local bank, the sheriff, and the town—and he thinks he owns the sensuous saloon singer, Charity, as well. But the moment Bolt and Charity eye each other there's fire—especially gunfire!

**#14: VIRGINIA CITY VIRGIN**                    (1360, $2.25)

When Katie's bawdy house holds a high stakes raffle, Bolt figures to take a chance. It's winner take all—and the prize is a budding nineteen year old virgin! But there's a passle of gun-toting folks who'd rather see Bolt in a coffin than in the virgin's bed!

**#15: BORDELLO BACKSHOOTER**                    (1411, $2.25)

Nobody has ever seen the face of curvaceous Cherry Bonner, the mysterious madam of the bawdiest bordello in Cheyenne. When Bolt keeps a pimp with big ideas and a terrible temper from having his way with Cherry, gunfire flares and a gambling man would bet on murder: Bolt's!

**#16: HARDCASE HUSSY**                    (1513, $2.25)

Traveling to set up his next bordello, Bolt is surrounded by six prime ladies of the evening. But just as Bolt is about to explore this lovely terrain, their stagecoach is ambushed by the murdering Beeler gang, bucking to be in Bolt's position!